The Swaddling Cloth

The Swaddling Cloth

Nan Pamer

WORD AFLAME PRESS

The Swaddling Cloth

by Nan Pamer

©2007, Word Aflame Press
Hazelwood, MO 63042-2299

Cover Design by Laura Jurek

Unless otherwise indicated, all quotations of Scripture are from the King James Version.

All rights reserved. No portion of this publication may be reproduced, stored in an electronic system, or transmitted in any form or by any means, electronic, mechanical, photocopy, recording, or otherwise, without the prior permission of Word Aflame Press. Brief quotations may be used in literary reviews.

Printed in United States of America

Printed by

WORD AFLAME PRESS
8855 Dunn Road, Hazelwood, MO 63042
www.pentecostalpublishing.com

Library of Congress Cataloging-in-Publication Data

Pamer, Nan.-
   The swaddling cloth : a Christmas story / by Nan Pamer.
     p. cm.
   ISBN 978-1-56722-718-5
   1. Christmas stories. I. Title.
   PS 3616.A357S93 2007
   813'.6—dc22
                                                          2007032171

Dedicated to our precious granddaughters:

Halle Maria Danes
Jesse Sullivan Pamer

Contents

	Introduction	9
1.	Riel	11
2.	Jude	25
3.	The Innkeeper and His Daughter	33
4.	Kira	41
5.	The Women at the Well	49
6.	Saagi	57
7.	The Marketplace Merchants	69
8.	Jude and Michal	79
9.	Michal and Riel	97
10.	Ben-Jared	109
11.	Mary and Joseph	119
12.	The Christ Child	125
13.	Kings of the East	143
14.	Riel and Jude	151
	Afterword	171

Introduction

Every Christmas, throughout the world, people gather for the retelling of the Christmas story. It never grows tiresome, and it commands the interest of the very young and the very old. How could a two-thousand-year-old story continue to interest such a wide range of people and do so, year after year?

Whether it is told through a church Christmas play, in a million-dollar production, or by a father simply opening the family Bible and reading the blessed narrative, the Christmas story never fails to quiet the heart and soothe the mind. Everything grows still at the telling of Christ's birth. A stable, a star, shepherds, wise men, angels, and a baby in a manger: they transcend all of time. Yes, the hush of the miraculous still hovers over the story of Christmas.

There are at least two ways to write about the events of our Savior's birth. Some writers choose a scholarly approach with all its careful attention to details. *When did the wise men come? Was it the actual night of Christ's birth, or was it two years later? How many wise men were there: two, three, ten? How old was Mary? Where was her family?* All these discussions have merit and certainly give honor to the story.

The second approach is completely different and is the basis of this book. The motivation of this story is simply to capture again that awe and wonder of Christmas. It is based upon that longing that I had as a child; what would it have been like to be at the manger? I have approached

The Swaddling Cloth

the story with some poetic license that reflects the way the story is often told. I trust you will feel again the wonder of Christmas.

Riel (Ri-EL)

The earth was returning to its ancient beginning hue, gray. A thousand variations of gray, but gray nonetheless. At the end of each day, this colorless cloak lay upon the earth until darkness took dominion. It was a humbling experience for the brilliant earth but a necessary part of life. There had to be rest. The light had to go out. Life could not be all sunshine. The graying earth was the perfect setting for weary and worn workers plodding their way home. They were tired, and the colorless dusk was soothing to their eyes.

Riel noticed all the fading of the earth as she walked, but at the sweet and vibrant age of seventeen, there was no plodding for her. Her steps were light and quick even under a heavy burden.

Riel paused and looked across the quiet, gentle hills of Judea. They were all she had ever known. The brown

The Swaddling Cloth

dust of the land clung to her feet and ankles almost unseen, for her skin was the color of the land.

The last breezes of the day blew gently over the land. The wind sang a peaceful melody. Riel watched the sun glowing in the western sky, hovering just above the horizon. The tranquil beauty of the scene seemed to slow the beat of her heart.

As a child of those hills, Riel had inherited their gentle yet steadfast nature, not always understanding the storm that whirled around her but remaining solid and immovable whatever the circumstance. She was as much a part of the land as the grass, the trees, and the soil.

Riel sighed as her brown eyes followed the silhouette of the hills against the darkening sky. Though young, she already sensed that they revealed the patterns of life. There were times of good and there were times of bad, and one must accept the inevitable of life to survive.

This was the land of Rachel, wife of the patriarch Jacob. Rachel had tasted both joy and sorrow. This parcel of land had become home to Ruth, the Moabitess. She had gleaned in Boaz's fields before becoming his wife. She was acquainted with loss and gain. The revered King David knew both the peaks and the valleys of this land and of life itself. This was the land of Judea, the city of Bethlehem—only a Sabbath's day's journey from the holy city of Jerusalem. It was the land of Riel.

"I will lift up mine eyes unto the hills," she quoted solemnly with tenderness and awe. Her respect for the land knew no bounds.

"As King David loved the hills, so do I," she breathed. "And as he loved his God, so do I." She prayed for several minutes with tears of joy at the thought of Him.

Riel (Ri-EL)

Just as quickly as her thoughts turned to God, they swung back to the realization that the daylight was slipping away. She raised her hand to steady the clay vessel atop her shoulder as she resumed walking.

Youthful thoughts could easily flow from the serious to the lighthearted.

"Stand tall and straight, my friend," she exclaimed to the stoic pot. "We have lots of water to carry, and it would be very difficult to carry it without you," Riel teased as she patted the cool sides of the pot, her mind snapping quickly to the job at hand.

Riel had mastered the fine art of balancing burdens; thus she had been assigned the job of bringing water to the inn from the community well.

"All those basins. . . ." she muttered, thinking of the work ahead.

Riel's graceful figure moved along the well-worn road. Her job had developed poise in her movements, giving her a regal bearing. But she boasted no royal lineage. She was simply a servant at the inn of Bethlehem.

Her head remained fixed, but her eyes flew across the landscape, taking in the beauty of the hills. She never missed a thing. Her eyes hungrily sought activity.

Riel crested a steep hill on the road and unexpectedly came face to face with a neighboring family. Riel had learned early in life that most adults ignore children and youths, but that did not stop her eternal optimism. Not once in her many encounters on the road did she fail to search the faces for a kind look. She did not watch for beauty or ugliness in their countenance, newness or shabbiness of their robes, nor the presence or absence of gold ornaments. Riel searched their eyes for kindness.

The Swaddling Cloth

Riel opened her mouth to speak. "Your barley fields . . ." she began wanting to congratulate them on the fruitfulness of their crops.

The mother, with a startled yet stern look, turned her face from Riel and looked into the distance. The rest of the family passed without a greeting.

At one point the father raised his eyes toward Riel, but she knew the expression. She had seen it many times since she had been reduced to a servant. Looking but not seeing, gazing through a person as though she did not exist, he was looking at the field behind Riel.

Riel sighed and spoke to the wind, for no one else was listening, ". . . were so beautiful this spring."

Like every other human, Riel longed for significance—she wanted to be recognized by her fellow man. It was not an ugly, arrogant lust for attention. She simply needed to know that a few people on earth knew she existed.

"Why some people would choose not to talk is indeed a mystery! I go to the well every day! I know things about their households they would love to know," she chuckled, pressing her lips together and trying to stifle the hurt of being ignored.

Ahead in the distance, Riel's sharp eyes caught sight of more people approaching. Two large figures led the group. Recognition dawned on Riel's face, causing her to drop her gaze. "Roman soldiers," she muttered softly, her mouth twisting down at the corners. She had encountered many at the inn, and they were usually condescending and cruel. Just as Riel raised her veil to cover her face, she saw a family trudging behind the men of war.

"Oh, that poor family," she sympathized.

Riel (Ri-EL)

The father and son carried the heavy burdens of the soldiers while the females of the family followed. It was a humiliating practice initiated by Rome. Jewish men were required to carry the belongings of a Roman soldier for a mile. Often, soldiers were neither tired nor in need of help with their burdens, but they delighted in tormenting the people of Judea. A mixture of fear and defiance permeated every Jew's interaction with the Romans.

"It's a shepherd's family," she exclaimed under her breath, immediately recognizing the style of robes and staffs the father and son carried.

Riel kept her eyes down, avoiding the men, but she could not keep her ears from hearing. "I broke his legs as easily as a stick of wood," the soldier bragged to his companion as the group drew closer. Riel heard the rough exchange and shuddered. She hated the violence of Rome. The men did not glance her way, but four sets of eyes looked on Riel with tenderness.

Once the soldiers passed, Riel turned to look at the family. No member of the shepherd's family spoke, lest attention be drawn to the lone girl whom the soldiers had chosen to ignore. But their kind eyes spoke volumes to Riel, and warmth flooded her heart. Had she been a queen, she would have given them half her kingdom for their kindness. She could only give them the most intense look of admiration and tuck their attention in a corner of her heart to savor at another time.

"Thank God for shepherds," she smiled. Perhaps their kindness was because they spent so many solitary hours in the hills. Those who led the flocks never seemed to take human companionship for granted.

Human kindness was a treasure to Riel. With the

smile sealed on her dark brown lips, she reached the favorite part of her journey, the back trail to the inn. The water pot did not feel as heavy as before.

The inn of Bethlehem sat on the top of a sloping hill, facing the south, and had a well-worn, winding path that connected with the main road. This wide tract of hardened earth led to the front entrance of the inn and was used by guests and visitors. But if one were coming from the town of Bethlehem, which was due north of the inn, it was quite a distance out of the way to go completely around the hill and come in the front entrance. Consequently the servants had devised a shortcut to the back of the inn to reduce their travel to town.

Thick, late-summer foliage covered the trees through this area of her walk, and she loved it. The cool feeling of the shade, the variegated green color, and the smell of the thick forest pleased her senses.

Upon reaching the clearing that led to the back door of the inn, she heard the lowing of the animals in the stable. Because opportunity rarely provided companions her age, she had found a variety of companions in the stable, especially younger animals.

"I don't think anyone will die of thirst," she reasoned and sat the pot near the back door of the inn. Her feet flew to the stable.

Part of the inn's stable consisted of a cave that was halfway down the hill to the east. Protruding from the top of the cool and dark lair were wooden beams, attached to thin poles stripped of their branches. This overhang extended the size of the shelter. Strung between the beams were mats of mud and grass. From the sides of the cave, a fence of rough-hewn timbers formed an outside enclosure that gave the animals some freedom to roam.

"Hello, my friends!"

In a manner that might have surprised an onlooker, the animals responded.

The ox turned his thick neck and gazed, the donkey stomped and snorted, and the sheep, en masse, moved toward the young woman, giving her their undivided attention.

"You look awfully worn today," she called to the ox and donkey inside the stable as she reached through the fence, touching the sheep she adored.

The feel of the wool delighted her. Since coming to the inn she had learned to weave. Her many hours on the loom, weaving wool into cloth, had deepened her affection for the sweet, little animals who made it possible for her to be warm in winter.

"Hello, little lambies," she cooed. "How were the green pastures today?"

Riel looked quickly to the left and right to make sure no one was watching. With one graceful bound, she jumped the fence. At seventeen, she was too old for such behavior, some of the older women might say, but childhood was so fresh in her mind. The endless delight of running, jumping, and climbing beckoned her throughout the day, and sometimes she had to respond.

She leaned close to their black noses, and they raised their wooly faces to her.

Beauty was dawning on the young woman's face, but she was unaware of it. Her heart-shaped face now had grown to fit her features. However, the placement of her features was not the full explanation for her beauty. A gentleness glowed in her countenance. It was one of those mysteries in the human condition—an inner beauty that comes from the spirit and emanates through the eyes and face. It can be seen but never explained.

Riel had that beauty, but she had no idea that it existed.

"And what did all of you sweet darlings do today?" she queried in jest. "Ate grass, then ate grass, . . . then ate grass?"

As she spoke she petted the noses of the sheep within her reach. The wooly creatures were pleased to have Riel in their midst.

One of the lambs pushed his way through the flock more determinedly than the rest. It was Broody. He was easy to spot because Riel had woven for him a thin collar of purple-dyed wool. He wore it proudly.

Riel laughed as she saw his small body squirming to her side. Broody was her favorite, and he knew it. Having been born in late spring and being somewhat of a runt, he was easily scooped into her arms.

"My little friend," she pressed the side of her face to his, "you missed me today, didn't you? I missed you, too!"

She leaned against the gatepost, holding the lamb, and simply enjoyed the sound and beauty of the animals. The other sheep soon dispersed as Riel continued petting Broody. Two adult sheep were nuzzling one another, and the action caught her attention.

"Oh, yes, love is in the stable," she smiled.

It was a curious sight to her because a longing for love and companionship had awakened in Riel. However, she knew there was little chance of a young Israelite male choosing her for a wife. She had nothing to give. She sighed softly at the thought of her lot in life but quickly

Riel (Ri-EL)

dismissed it from her mind. Hugging the lamb tightly, she glanced at the grayness of the valley that stretched below the stable.

"Oh, come on! We have a few minutes."

Hurrying to the gate and still holding Broody, she slipped through, using her knee to prevent the other sheep from following.

"Can I take Broody for a little run?" she cried to Josiah, who stepped from inside the stable just as she was shutting the rough gate.

Josiah waved to Riel, nodding with understanding.

The old Israelite rested his gnarled hand against the rough rock at the entrance of the cave, watching Riel as she gently placed Broody on the grassy hillside. The girl and the lamb broke into a full run.

"Jehovah, life never saw fit to give me a family, yet You in mercy have brought this child into my life. I thank You." Tears welled up in the elder's eyes.

Josiah smiled and thought of the first time he had seen the little, bright-eyed Riel. Her shy and gentle nature had drawn the old man's heart right to hers.

Now the sound of laughter drifted up the hill, and he smiled, shaking his head. "Poor Broody!" Josiah knew the little lamb would try to keep up with Riel, regardless of how hard she ran.

Riel had reached the low point of the valley where a little stream flowed. In one swift bound she was over it, and she stopped and turned to wave at Josiah.

He raised his hand in acknowledgment but turned to go back inside the stable. He knew Riel would wave as long as he stood watching.

She glanced each way, surveying the beauty. The valley

The Swaddling Cloth

was such great joy to her! It was completely surrounded by hills and only used as grazing places for the animals around Bethlehem. Seldom did anyone invade her sanctuary.

Her attention then turned again to the lamb that was slowly making his way through the stream. Riel turned and ran across the small valley. The wind whirled about her face, making her cheeks glow with health. Her eyes danced as she looked back to see if her lamb could keep pace. At the beginning of summer he was not able to stay up, but now he was almost her equal and she loved it.

The green grass beneath, the cool breeze of a summer's evening, and the love of a small animal made the heart of the young orphan sing, and her voice gave the feeling words.

Her laughter and song rang throughout the hills that surrounded her special valley. The moment her feet touched the cool grass of the low ground, she was no longer a slave.

She fell to her knees and playfully pushed Broody's nose. He swung his head away to get out of her grasp and then returned for her to push him away again. It was a little game they both enjoyed.

Riel leaned back on her hands and waited for her heart to slow its pace. Pulling her head covering off so that she might better feel the wind, she glanced instinctively in the direction of the inn that was hidden by a thick grove of trees.

"I know I have lots of water to pour, but I will stay just another minute," she said and lay back, looking at the sky. Darkness was beginning to spread.

"Because thy lovingkindness is better than life, my lips shall praise thee."

Riel (Ri-EL)

She looked into the clear sky and thought of life and love. She knew it was the mercy of God that she was alive, and she was ever grateful for life. But in the area of love, she had her doubts that even God could bring a man to love her. In Israel, children were espoused to a mate very early in life, and no such thing had happened to Riel.

"My faith is in You, Lord. You will lead me. . . . No young Israelite male will ever be interested in me," she sighed, realizing her doubt in spite of her faith.

"Orphans that have no support are hardly a prize!" she reasoned. Often she had this conversation with God. She longed for the love of just one man, but with her circumstances, she knew it was nearly impossible.

"I plan to dwell in the courts of Your temple in Jerusalem, O God, praying and fasting all my days, as soon as I can find someone who knows the high priest," she resigned, knowing that this too was in the realm of impossibilities.

High on a hill looking down on Riel's meadow, a lone, young shepherd stood watching. All through the spring and summer months of that year, he had watched the girl who loved the lamb. She emanated life even from a distance. His soul was drawn to her though he did not know her nor had he spoken one word to her. Early in his childhood, he had felt the call to love the Judean hills, and there was no doubt that this girl felt it, too. It was this love that first caught his attention. The little romps of the girl and the lamb had amused him and broke up the monotony of the shepherd's life, but then it drew him.

The Swaddling Cloth

Her gentle playfulness with the lamb began to touch him deeply. If one could have peered into the young shepherd's heart, he would have seen love igniting.

The young shepherd's name was Jude.

He shifted his shepherd's robe, one of particularly fine cloth, and began prodding his flock with the crook of his staff to stay away from the edge of the cliff while his eyes stayed on the young woman in the meadow. It was getting so dark he could hardly make out her tall slender form. His eyes, as sharp as an eagle's, could barely see the purple ring around the lamb's neck.

"Well, you are late again," he teased her from afar, holding his staff up as though he were making a point.

With complete honesty he spoke because he knew she could not hear, "I've longed to see you throughout the day." His heart swelled with feelings with which he was unfamiliar.

Riel's laughter wafted across the land on the wind. Jude strained his ear to hear every sound of it. He loved the girl, and he had never met her.

Riel, completely unaware that she was being watched, began making her way out of the valley. The singing and laughter stopped, and Jude watched as she led the lamb back to the fold. He did not take his eyes from her until she completely disappeared from his sight.

Jude leaned heavily on his staff, gripping it with hard, calloused hands. He knew night was near, but he could not bring himself to leave until he was absolutely sure she would not return.

"She's not a servant; she walks free. She must be the innkeeper's daughter," he spoke as softly as the night air.

Immediately, his fears voiced themselves, "What if

she is betrothed to someone else?"

The thought caused a pain deep in his chest, and he reacted by turning swiftly from the valley, calling his flock, and forcing his mind to the task that was immediately at hand.

But the image of the girl running with the lamb stole back into his mind within minutes. "I must speak to my father. I must!" Jude declared to his disinterested flock.

"What do you fear? Where is the blood of the lion of Judah that courses through your veins?" he scolded himself and then laughed. He knew he would tremble before that girl.

Because the shepherd's life gave few opportunities to follow all customs of the day, there had been no choice made for a mate for Jude. While most of his friends in the city were espoused to a mate, he was not.

Jude roughly rubbed the back of his neck. "Betrothals would make life much easier." But when he considered his feelings toward the girl who ran across the meadows with a lamb, Jude was thankful to God that he could make his own choice.

"I do not fear the lion or the bear," he fumed. "Why do I fear this?"

The sheep were getting restless as they sensed the coming darkness.

"Home!" he commanded as the girl made her way back to the inn. The flock, as if in one mind, headed back to their fold with their shepherd leading the way.

2
Jude

Something mystical happens when boys become men. Through childhood, they are told what to do by anyone their elder. Then sometime during the year right before manhood, seemingly overnight, they develop an air of confidence that transforms them. They are given respect without demanding it. Men and women, who have known them as boys all their lives, give the young men a place in conversation that was never given before.

Jude had reached that point in life, and he was uneasy with his newfound honor.

As the son of Ben-Jared, the leading shepherd of Bethlehem, Jude had seen his father's flocks swell to huge numbers. Though born in poverty, Ben-Jared was now a wealthy man, and the honor that wealth brings was extended to his son.

Quick wealth can sometimes destroy people, but the

The Swaddling Cloth

house of Ben-Jared held wise men who knew wealth could leave as quickly as it came. This family chose to remember the "day of small things." Ben-Jared did not gravitate to the people of wealth in the cities of Judah, though he would have been received with open arms. Rather, he stayed with his own kind, the shepherds, and for this he was greatly revered.

Jude walked toward a cluster of tents encamped at the base of a hill. The tents were pitched at the edge of a green pasture, beside a swift brook. It was a choice piece of land recently purchased by Ben-Jared for a large sum of money. Judah rarely had choice land for sale, but Ben-Jared, a persistent negotiator, patiently bargained and got what he wanted.

"I've stayed out too long," Jude chastened himself. He knew there would be questions and hated the thought of that, but the residue of joy that lingered from seeing the girl made it all seem worthwhile.

Opening the gate to the sheepfold, he called for the flock. They were already stumbling over one another to get into the rough-hewn enclosure they knew as home. The sheep called out greetings to the other flocks, making a commotion that Jude knew would draw attention to his lateness.

Loud laughter, the sound of music, and singing filled the night. The other shepherds gathered with their extended families in the large central tent, where the food was prepared and served. Each evening all the members of the Ben-Jared family came to talk of the day's events.

Jude felt the pangs of hunger, but his dread of being in the crowd of inquisitive family overcame his pain.

Jude

I hope Mother has brought something to my tent. I'll look there first, he reasoned in himself. He stole quietly toward his own tent, avoiding the small fires burning at many of the tents' doors, hoping not to be noticed.

The young shepherd had developed a strong dislike for one trapping of wealth that Ben-Jared could not avoid. Because of the huge number of flocks, his father had to deal with many new people, and Jude's life was now filled with strangers. Jude was extremely uncomfortable with the obsequious way that many of these adults treated him. At times they acted as if he were a prince. Grown men who bowed when he entered and hung over his every word unsettled Jude, who had been taught from infancy that humility pleased God and that pride was as destructive as a plague. So Jude avoided these people. He reached his tent and quickly pulled back the badger-skin door.

"Jude, you startled me!" his mother smiled while placing her hand over her heart. She was relieved to see him.

"I'm sorry, Mother," he spoke sincerely and then in humor. "Darkness comes so quickly. I am so hungry I could eat the tent!"

"Young shepherds stay hungry," Otha shook her head as she hurriedly placed bread and cheese on a clean cloth for him.

"Eat, eat," she commanded while she chose flawless figs from the small baskets of fruit the servants had brought back from the marketplace.

Jude paused, thinking of the goodness of God for providing every need for their family.

As he reached to tear a piece of bread, his mother laid her hand on his shoulder. "Jude, are you at peace?"

The Swaddling Cloth

"Yes, I believe I am," he replied after a pause, looking into her loving eyes.

"Your father has noticed you no longer come to the big tent with the others. He is concerned that you are troubled," she explained.

This godly mother of Israel could hear the sounds of the heart, and she knew there was unrest in her firstborn's heart without his saying a word.

Jude looked at his hands that were now clasped in his lap.

"Our lives have changed so much. Father once spent hours with me, teaching the law of God. Now there are so many people. . . ." His voice trailed off, completely avoiding the real reason for his turmoil.

He paused for a moment and then looked intently at her, "Mother, I hate the way some of the others light up when Father enters a room. It's as though he were a god!"

His straightforwardness pleased her, yet she knew she would do whatever she could to keep peace between her husband and son.

"You are right, but your father is a wise man. He knows the nature of men but is kind and patient with them," she explained in earnestness.

Jude longed to find his place in the world. He wanted to be esteemed by men of his equal, yet not like this! Not based upon the false accolades of lesser men who only loved the family's wealth. Such conduct was dishonorable in Israel, but so many fell prey to it. His righteous indignation felt good.

While Jude's thoughts and words spoke of his displeasure of the changing events in their lives, it was not the true cause of his discontentment. It was the girl.

Jude

"These things you will better understand when you are older. Now you must eat." Otha was careful with her tone. Since Jude's height now exceeded her own considerably, she did not speak to him in the same manner she did when he was a child.

Otha was puzzled by his words. She knew something more was wrong.

Just as Jude was finishing his meal, the handsome and rugged Ben-Jared entered the tent. In his thirty-eighth year, Ben-Jared was in the prime of his manhood. His height and his demeanor afforded him immediate respect.

Jude rose to his feet and bowed his head. "Father," he acknowledged reverently.

"Jude, I've been waiting for you. There are men from the tribe of Issachar here, and they want to purchase ewes. I wanted them to see your flock, and I want you to learn the art of trade." Ben-Jared paused as he studied the expression of this younger image of himself. His strong, brown fingers gripped the wooden staff, and he felt a strong impulse to pull Jude to himself with the crook of his staff as he would a straying lamb.

"Yes, Father," the youth replied, not raising his head. It was not as easy to be candid with his opinions with his father present. An awkward silence hung between them.

Ben-Jared leaned his staff against the tall, earthen pots of water. He ran his hand across the silken softness lining the inside of the tent, never forgetting the former days. It was much finer than the goat-haired coverings of the past. He adjusted his robe in silence and then spoke, "Son, why have you not come to the meeting tent?"

His father's no-nonsense countenance demanded truth, but Jude did not know the answer. He resented the men of the tent; he longed for the girl with the lambs. He wanted to be still; he wanted to run. He wanted to sing; he wanted to weep. How could he possibly express the storm that was raging inside him?

"I prefer the quietness of my mother's tent," he hated saying the words. They were technically true words, yet they were lame with deception and he knew they were not words Ben-Jared wanted to hear. Frankly, there was no place on earth that Jude would rather be than beside his father. His father's approval was extremely important to him.

"I'm sorry, Father. I will come to the tent now," he said earnestly with a tinge of rebellion born of frustration and not disrespect as he reached for his staff lying on the ground.

Ben-Jared's eyes narrowed at his son's response, but suddenly, deep in Ben-Jared's memory, a familiar chord struck. He understood. Jude had not said one word that told the turmoil in his heart, but somehow the father knew. He had walked the road. He did not know the details, but the uncertainty of those years at the brink of manhood came back to Ben-Jared and, for a brief moment, the waves of those memories washed over him. He had come to confront and scold his first-born son, but now he reached out and put his hand on his shoulder.

"It is important to understand the rules of trade, not just shepherding," Ben-Jared avoided the true subject as much as his son had, yet there was understanding that passed between the two men's spirits.

"Otha, we will return shortly," Ben-Jared spoke quietly as he caught his wife's eyes.

"I will be here when you return," she let his eyes hold

hers. "I will light the lamps and wait," she added. How she loved those two men in her life!

The Innkeeper and His Daughter

Bethlehem's inn was growing dark as Riel pushed open the back door of the newest addition to the inn. She filled her lungs with the scent of freshly cut wood and hardened mud as she quickly began filling the basins with water. One small lamp had been lit on a shelf on the wall.

Riel smiled, "Somebody is watching out for me."

This new room was large, built to accommodate the male travelers who stopped at the inn for rest. It had been added in the early spring due to the large numbers moving about the country. Caesar Augustus, the ruler of the Roman empire, had sent out a decree that every person must return to the land of his birth to be taxed. This was a heavy burden on the citizens of the country, but it was profitable for innkeepers. In the late watches of the night, when the innkeeper of the inn of Bethlehem counted his coins, he gleefully whispered his appreciation to the Caesar.

Before, there had been no place for women because they seldom traveled. However, since the new taxation regulations, the inn had been overflowing with men and women of every age. The old part of the inn now was for the women and children, and the new section was for the male travelers.

The inn consisted of four rooms.

Travelers entered the inn by way of the front room. They often warmed themselves by the fire as the temperatures began to cool. Also, because of the growing number of guests, this room served as the sleeping room for the innkeeper and his daughter. They slept among the piles of belongings brought in by the guests. When money comes quickly and easily, inconvenience means nothing, at least for a while. The ceiling was low and the walls were made of mud. A large table dominated the room and each evening guests gathered here for supper.

The two sleeping rooms for travelers extended off the east and west sides of this main room, and the remaining room was little more than a shed, where the food was stored and prepared by the servants. It was this room that Riel called home.

As Riel made her way quietly across the large new room, she could hear the men talking in low tones around the fire.

"Well, there are only two things that cause them to lower their voices, speaking against Caesar or telling of his sordid deeds," Riel mused.

Nathaniel snorted with delight as he sat at the head of the long, rough table. "The house of Caesar has the

The Innkeeper and His Daughter

morals of dogs!" He leaned forward with anticipation to hear the conclusion of the story. "The leaders of Rome are the vilest people on earth," he exclaimed in dismay, yet delight showed in his eyes that defied understanding.

Nathaniel leaned back for a moment while the conversation lulled. He then moved in closer as he recounted his favorite lewd story of Rome.

"Back in the spring, there was a son of Reuben who now lives in Rome. He had a daughter that Caesar took a fancy to, and he said what that girl had to endure." Nathaniel spoke low and uninterrupted.

Gossip was Nathaniel's favorite pastime. He often complained about the women with long tongues who gathered at the well, but he was of that same nature. Their gossip was about known townspeople; Nathaniel's was about unknown city people.

Nathaniel paused and looked at his daughter, Michal. "Michal, go see what is taking Kira and Riel so long with the food."

Michal sat on a low stool in the farthest corner from the others. She held her head in her hand while she stared gloomily across the room at the flames dancing above the burning wood.

"No!" she snapped at him. "They are lazy! That is why the food is late," she spoke with scorn and hardness.

Nathaniel ignored her rebellion and simply lowered his voice more and leaned closer to his listeners.

Nathaniel's weak, shallow nature did not show itself very often in dealing with the servants or the guests, but in his relationship with his daughter it was glaring. Michal had entered the world with a very strong will. Her strong will and Nathaniel's weakness were not a good combination.

The Swaddling Cloth

Michal's mother had died when she was very young, and her father yielded to his child's every whim. Early in life, he had tried to conquer her demanding, hard nature, but eventually he found it much easier to give in. Her strong will, if harnessed, could have served her well in dealing with the harshness of life, but uncontrolled it only ruined her. She had not learned to work, and her personality was warped because her uselessness.

Michal's beauty, added to her strong will and laziness, only increased warping of her character. Many of the travelers who stayed at the inn commented on her beauty, and because of it, her destructive qualities were overlooked. Most people chose to amuse her instead of correct her.

At a young age, Michal sensed the regard that adults had for her. Most children were ignored, but not Michal. When she was still a young child, her female relatives spoke admiringly of her beauty and never mentioned the attributes of the other children who were present. Silly adults who frequented the inn would praise her for trifling things and overlook the children playing with her. Very early, Michal noticed the distinction that was made between her and the other children. She soon had a unrealistic and exalted opinion of herself.

More travelers entered the door of the inn. Riel chose the same moment to fill the pitchers and basins. She placed the large urn on the floor and hurriedly began filling the various basins about the room.

Amidst the clamor of Nathaniel collecting Roman coins from the newest guests and the conversation that had resumed by the fire, Riel heard the angry voice of Michal call her.

The Innkeeper and His Daughter

"Riel, come here at once," Michal commanded. Riel groaned inwardly. She accepted the fact she was a servant, but Michal's haughtiness made her cringe. She walked quickly to Michal.

"Hello, Michal," Riel greeted her with genuine effort. "Do we have new guests tonight?"

Michal ignored her question.

"Where is the food, you fool? We are trying to run an inn here. People want to eat at the end of the day. You are always late. Stupid, stupid! What have you been doing?" Michal's spiteful complaint spewed from her lips.

"I dream of the day that Jehovah sends us some decent servants!" Michal turned her head and ended the conversation before giving Riel a chance to say anything. The ancient Jewish adage was true, "The fathers have eaten sour grapes, and the children's teeth are set on edge." Something about the ugliness of soul that was eating Nathaniel had been passed on to his child but with a deeper rottenness.

Riel stood quietly for a moment. While such cruelty brings out meanness in some, in others it produces a deep inferiority that touches every part of life. Riel felt the invisible blows of Michal's tongue, but she determined not to be affected by them in either way.

I will not be cruel and become like her. I will not become the nothing she wants to make of me, Riel breathed in the deepest recesses of her heart.

"Why are you just standing there?" Michal suddenly spit out. Her words were cold and low. No one could hear but her victim. The loud conversation of the guests kept Riel and Michal's conversation in complete privacy.

Riel's eyes dropped to the floor in submission, knowing

that was required of her. She said nothing.

Michal looked away again, fuming to herself, "Arrogant servants, what a curse! She thinks she is something beautiful and knows everything." Michal could never accept another girl's beauty or brightness of mind. She was determined to tear Riel down.

Riel was not the first to attract her attention. Every young woman who came in contact with the inn knew the wrath of Michal. Even servant girls, traveling with their masters, were fair game. Michal mentioned their disheveled clothes, a birthmark, the condition of their sandals—anything to draw attention to a flaw instead of the loveliness.

"I want you to prepare the eating utensils," Michal commanded.

Riel knew this was Michal's job but was happy to do it just to be away from her. The hatred Michal had for Riel was so real one could almost touch its ugliness.

Michal reached up and pinched Riel's arm as hard as she possibly could while twisting the skin. Tears came to Riel's eyes as the pain shot up her arm, but she did not move until Michal released her.

"Go!" Michal hissed.

Riel ran to the shelves at the far end of the room to be away from the torture. The cruelty was bewildering to her. Picking up the rough wooden bowls, Riel's quiet figure quickly carried them to the main table. She felt shame and embarrassment at the condescending words and the rough treatment of Michal.

A shy, young servant girl whose master frequented the inn suddenly appeared beside Riel. "Do not worry," she whispered. "We all call Michal, 'Queen of the Dunghill.'"

The Innkeeper and His Daughter

The desire of the girl to make Riel feel better touched her deeply. Tears glistened in the corners of Riel's eyes.

"Thank you," she softly responded, never looking at the girl lest she also incur Michal's wrath.

Even with the encouragement of the young peer, the words of Michal were like heavy blows, hurtful, humiliating, and frightening.

Riel smiled to herself. She had often heard the boys who helped clean the stable laugh about Michal and her harsh and haughty tongue.

"I swear that Caesar Augustus banished Michal to Bethlehem for trying to take his throne!" the stable hands often teased. The boys knew they could be whipped for laughing at the innkeeper's daughter, but it was the only way the servants knew how to counter Michal's attempt to make them feel insignificant.

What would I do if Michal made me leave? A gnawing fear knotted Riel's stomach, and she could hardly think of it without shaking in fear. She had no place else to go. The inn was her home. Despite Michal, Riel had found a haven, and she wanted to remain here.

Riel kept her head low as she finished preparing the table. She wanted to rub the throbbing place on her arm. However, she did not want to arouse more of Michal's anger, and the more lowly she acted, the less the "Queen" was irritated. Riel could not understand why the badgering from Michal had seemed to increase in the last month.

Just then, Josiah entered with a pot of soup and a large basket of bread.

The group stirred about, and conversations turned toward hunger as the aroma permeated the room. Riel could make her escape unnoticed. Riel knew there was

The Swaddling Cloth

one person in the world who could build up what Michal had tried to tear down. She was Kira.

Kira

Riel walked to the back of the room and pushed open the tanned animal skins that separated the area where the guests gathered from the area where the servants stayed. It was here, in this lean-to shed, that the food for the inn was prepared. Although it was only a few feet from Michal and the other people, Riel felt miles removed from them as soon as she entered this place. She opened to a wonderful world of aromas and a large fire crackling in the fireplace. The warm air mixing with the aroma of cooking meat and baking bread soothed her. The freshly baked bread cooling on the hearth and the second pot of vegetable pottage boiling turned Riel's attention from her hurting heart to her empty stomach.

Kira, the cook, was again kneading bread dough. It was an endless task at the inn. She was a precious mother of Israel whose faith in Jehovah had deeply affected Riel.

The Swaddling Cloth

Riel's father had taught her the laws of God, but children do not always adhere to the faith of their fathers when left to themselves. Providence had shown mercy to Riel in placing her with Kira.

Despair can make the walls of character fragile. Kira remembered how fragile those walls were in Riel when she had knocked at the inn's door seven years ago. She had set about reinforcing those walls of Riel's life. The love of an old woman had held the girl together and taught Riel to laugh again.

Riel flew across the room and threw her arms around Kira's plump body. The smell of leaven and flour permeated the old cook, and the younger woman drank in the smell.

"Kira, your bread is pure manna, the bread of angels!" she exclaimed as she let go of Kira. Riel leaned over and plucked a crumb from the edge of a loaf. Her voice was cheerful, yet if you listened closely you could discern a hint of the pain she still felt in her heart.

Kira stopped her kneading and looked lovingly at Riel as she made her way to the hearth. The old woman was so proud of the graceful and spirited girl.

Riel sat down beside a row of loaves cooling on the hearth. She slowly rubbed her pinched skin. The slant of her shoulders and the hurt in her eyes told Kira something had gone wrong.

Kira spoke softly as she talked to Riel and pushed back a strand of hair with her forearm, "Well, my little lamb, you remind me of a little flower in great need of water."

Riel smiled weakly and raised her shoulders. Kira always could read her heart by her posture.

"Oh, Michal continues on her mission to make me feel as low as she possibly can."

Kira

Kira replied tenderly, "Sit down. Some hot, spicy soup will revive you, and God will mend your spirit." She had observed Michal's spiteful behavior toward Riel on many occasions. But Kira knew that as servants, they could do nothing to stop it. She had hoped the girl would grow tired of tormenting Riel.

"Kira, I don't know what I would do without you." Riel's voice drifted off to a whisper.

Kira's old and slow body moved to wrap her arms around the thin frame of the young woman.

"Jehovah has brought us together. In this lonely world of endless work, we are so blessed to have one another."

The warm soup and the good company managed to raise Riel's spirits somewhat, and she sat talking with Kira, telling her of the meanness of Michal.

"Perhaps you feel like weaving tonight by the fireside," Kira suggested.

Riel smiled. That was always Kira's answer to pain—weaving. But Riel knew it was a valuable lesson in life and she had submitted to the learning. Since Riel had come to the inn as a little orphan, Kira had taught Riel to pour her sorrow into something. Though a child, Riel had sensed the profound wisdom of the exercise and had quickly given herself to it.

Kira held a simple philosophy of life. Sorrow is going to come. It will try to paralyze a person, but if one can learn to channel sorrow into good, sorrow has lost its power to harm. If fact, wonderful things can be accomplished. At the end of the difficult time, if the sorrow has been poured into some labor, it is a blessing instead of a curse.

From the very beginning of Riel's time at the inn, when grief came over the loss of her former life, Kira

The Swaddling Cloth

would sit her at the loom and teach her to weave the wool into cloth. In the seven years that she had lived with Kira, whenever sadness came, she had woven wool. The woolen clothes she had made served them well. Riel discovered the great treasure of Kira's simple philosophy.

Along with teaching her to weave, Kira had admonished her to pray. "Jehovah hears and He answers," Kira repeated these words over and over until Riel became convinced that prayer was important. Riel took everything to God while she poured her sorrow into the loom.

Riel patted Kira's hand and gently said, "As soon as I finish cleaning up after the guests, I will weave."

Kira smiled, happy that Riel had learned the important lesson of life. "No. No, child. Tonight I will go in and clean up after the meal. You have walked and worked all day. You need a rest. Nathaniel will not notice."

Riel was too exhausted to argue, and the prospect of avoiding Michal was irresistible.

"Thank you, Kira," she spoke with her head down, with deep gratitude in her voice as she walked to the loom.

"And," Kira glowed, "I have a surprise for you!"

Riel looked down and noticed a new sack beside the loom. She reached down and thrust her hand into the soft bundle.

"Oh, Kira, why didn't you tell me? This must be Broody's wool! Josiah told me it was almost dry. I knew his wool would be soft, but I never realized it was quite like this!" she exclaimed. "I will make something very special with it, I will," Riel determined. "I knew that lamb was special the first time I saw him. Remember, Kira, how tiny he was when he was born?" she reminisced.

"Yes, I remember the little lamb," Kira's mind went

Kira

back to the early spring. "He wouldn't have made it if you had not cared for him."

"He is the sweetest, most gentle lamb we've had, isn't he?" Riel asked, knowing the answer.

"Oh, he is! He is!" replied the old cook, who had seen many lambs born.

The wool had been washed and dried, and all the knots combed from it. It was ready to be woven into a soft and delicate cloth.

"Josiah brought it in today," explained Kira as she was putting the last of the loaves of bread in the small oven. "He was determined that the bundle of Broody's wool belong to you."

A tender smile again broke onto Riel's face. "God bless that precious man." Her heart welled up with thanksgiving for the two kind people in her life.

Weaving wool into cloth was the one job at the inn that Riel did not consider work. Holding the wool, stretching it across the loom, and being in control of where it was going was comfort somehow. She quickly prepared the crude weaving structure and began feeding the soft wool into it. Riel's love for the sheep was also seen in her enjoyment of working with their wool.

As she lit an oil lamp she hummed a little Jewish lullaby her mother had sung to her as a child. The melody took her mind back to her parents. They had died seven years earlier from a mysterious fever. Riel was ten years old at the time, an only child, and there had been no one to share her pain and loss.

Her parents were shepherds and had lived on the Judean hills in tents several miles from Bethlehem. It was not an easy life for a child, but a happy one. Her

The Swaddling Cloth

parents had loved each other, and both had loved her. The fever that had stuck her parents was quick and deadly. Between two Sabbaths, she lost both of them. A neighboring shepherd had come, taken the sheep, and made arrangements with the innkeeper for Riel to live at the inn. For reasons she did not understand, there was no family to come to her aid. She remembered the shepherd asking her if she had a kinsman redeemer, but Riel did not know what that meant. Her little family had kept to themselves with their small flock and she knew nothing of her extended family, if she even had one. Her parents had never mentioned relatives.

Riel paused at the loom for a moment. Her mind wandered back to those days of sleeping under the stars on warm summer nights. During those days the Judean hills had stolen her heart. She remembered sitting on the cool grass with her parents, watching the stars, and listening to the lowing of the sheep. It was the most blessed time of her life, and regardless of the hardships she now experienced working in the inn, those memories were beautiful and precious and they softened the most severe blows.

Then, in the midst of memories, her mind went to prayer. She thanked God for all that He done for her: His watchful care, His tender mercies.

She worked and wove and prayed as the guests in the next room grew more boisterous.

She worked and wove and prayed as they moved from the table to the fire.

She worked and wove and prayed as they chattered and strove to impress each other.

She worked and wove and prayed as they moved to their mats to sleep.

Kira

She worked and wove and prayed until the oil in her lamp was gone out.

Riel made her way to the corner of the shed, where she and Kira kept their sleeping mats. Riel could tell that Kira was already asleep by the steady rhythm of her breathing. She looked at her darkened form and thought of the two people in the world who cared for her, Kira and Josiah. She loved them dearly.

She sighed softly as she knelt beside her mat. Her last thoughts of the day were: *O God, thank You for the bountiful blessings You have given me, and please direct my steps.* A sweet aroma went up to God as she fell into a restful sleep.

Later that night, the pains that come with age awakened Kira and she looked at the place where Riel lay. She reached out and tenderly patted Riel's shoulder.

A prayer slipped heavenward, "What a precious gift You have given to all of us. Give me wisdom to lead her in the right paths. Let me know the right time to explain things to her that she needs to know. Give us both courage, God; courage for me to make her understand and courage for her to accept it."

5
The Woman at the Well

Early the next morning just before dawn, the birds' sweet song called to all those who had things to do. Riel answered their call. Every morning brought renewed vigor to her. Past hurts and disappointments faded, and she began again. Michal's contempt did not seem so overwhelming after a night of rest.

For a few moments, she lay on her mat trying to remember the details of her dreams. She had been walking the hills of Judea with a young man. Everything was peaceful and beautiful in her dream, but she could not see his face. She replayed the dream over and over in her mind so she wouldn't forget it. Suddenly she realized that time was slipping away, and she rose to begin the duties of the day.

Riel quickly rolled up her mat and slipped her outer garment over her head. The light wool felt good in the

The Swaddling Cloth

coolness of the room. She ran a comb through her hair and twisted it into a knot at the nape of her neck. Carrying her sandals and hoping not to awaken Kira, she made her way out of the food room with one of the clay pots in her arm.

Quietly entering the room where the female travelers slept, she began her morning chores of filling pitchers and basins. Though the room was dark, Riel could make out two women sitting on their mats, braiding their long hair. Riel bowed, acknowledging them, but no one said a word, not wanting to awaken the others. Next she made her way to the new room, which was packed full of men, all sleeping. Snores of every sort filled the room.

"What a noise!" Riel laughed to herself.

There were several basins and pitchers to fill, requiring her to make several trips to the food room, where she stored her filled pots of water on the hearth of the fireplace.

As she reentered the room, the cacophony of snores reached such a pitch that Riel could hardly stifle her laughter. "How can anyone sleep?" she wondered. While many of those who stayed in the inn were condescending to the servants like Riel, hearing this loud and comical snoring somehow evened out the differences. It was hard to feel inferior to someone who made these kinds of noises!

"I wonder if that handsome young man in my dreams makes that abominable noise when he sleeps?" Riel laughed and shook her head. Her mind went back to the dream and lingered for just a moment as she finished the last of the basins.

As the sun splashed light and shadows through the hills, awakening every part of nature, Riel had her water pot balanced on her shoulder and was headed toward the well. She reached the edge of the inn's clearing and heard the familiar bleating of the sheep as Josiah led them off to graze.

"Oh, how I love that sight!" she exclaimed as she watched the skilled shepherd lead the flock across the valley. She wanted to call out a greeting to Josiah and thank him for the wool, but she did not want to disturb the guests and especially not Nathaniel or Michal. She sat her pot down and waved vigorously though she knew there was little chance of Josiah seeing her.

With her hand still raised, Riel was overwhelmed by the beauty of the vista before her. The sun rising over the hills, the sky filled with glowing colors, the gentle flock making their way across the valley caused Riel's eyes to fill with tears.

This was the land where the patriarchs and their wives were buried, and somehow she sensed their presence. Riel felt her connection to all of her forefathers when she gazed at the distant hills. Their dust now mingled with the land.

"What beauty! What a wonderful world!" she sighed as she directed her words to the Maker of the morning.

King David, the most revered of all the kings of Israel and Judah, was often in Riel's thoughts and prayers. Many times, Kira had told her the stories of his life. David's love for the sheep was a love she could easily understand, and she knew he had often walked these hills. The fact that he had been an insignificant part of his family, unappreciated by his father and brothers, made her feel like the ancient king was a kindred spirit. As God had taken care of David, He would take care of Riel—she believed this with all her heart.

The beauty of the hills never got old. As Riel sat on

the cool grass, she untwisted her hair and let it hang loose, feeling the morning breeze playfully dance about her. Her gaze was fixed on Josiah and the sheep. She felt the pangs of morning hunger and decided to eat the crust of bread she had grabbed as the flock moved farther away. They became one flowing form, moving to the distant pasture while led by the shepherd.

"I am so glad to be here, Jehovah," she prayed. "Forgive me for complaining and grieving about a few imperfect things in my life. Jehovah, I thank You for everything I have, for the chance to live in the inn, and for Kira and Josiah. Please help me with Michal. I know she hates me, and I don't know why. She makes me feel worthless, but I know that You care for me. I'm so happy about that."

She looked across the hills at the bright sun and smiled as though God Himself were shining out of it. Her time in prayer was the final thrust to put Riel back in the enjoyment of life and work. She twisted up her hair quickly and neatly, replaced her head covering, and in one graceful, flowing movement, she lifted her water pot and started toward the road to the well.

Riel enjoyed her time at the well while waiting for her turn. There were servants coming and going continuously in the early hours of the days. In a few moments' time, one could learn enormous amounts of news about what was going on in the community around Bethlehem. Most of the servants who carried water were women. Here they felt a freedom to be themselves. There was never a shortage of conversation. As she approached the familiar well area, she could hear the chatter of the women servants. This morning the group consisted of servants whom Riel did not know very well. However,

The Women at the Well

Riel soon discovered that while she did not know this group by name, they too talked about a staple subject of the regular water-carriers—betrothals. No bride and groom in the land of Judea knew their future as well as the women at the well! Today, a new name was being discussed, one that Riel had never heard before, Jude.

"He has grown into such a handsome young man, just like his father," one large woman was proclaiming to all who would listen. She beamed as she looked around to see who was giving her their attention. To her delight, several faces turned toward her.

Riel took her place at the end of the line and called a greeting to Reuba, a servant girl from the house of Dan who carried water to the marketplace in Bethlehem. Riel said no more, for like everyone else, she wanted to hear what the woman had to say. She sat her pot down in the long row, and though Riel looked away, her ear was toward the woman.

"I'm sure he will be making his choice of a bride soon. My Ben told me he overheard Ben-Jared, our master, and his wife, Otha, discussing it," she raised her shoulders and crossed her arms across her broad chest, gloating at her audience.

Reuba slipped in line beside Riel and explained, "They are servants of Ben-Jared, the wealthy shepherd who has recently moved his flocks among the Judean hills close by. His servants have just started using Bethlehem's well and the marketplaces. Only when his wells are low or the flocks have clouded the water do his servants come to Bethlehem's well."

Riel had recently heard his name mentioned in the marketplace. At one point, Ben-Jared had sought the

The Swaddling Cloth

counsel of the elders in the city concerning grazing areas for his large flocks. He was respected by the citizens of Bethlehem.

While every woman at the well was a servant, there still remained a system of hierarchy. Those who worked for the wealthy people were treated with higher esteem by all the other servants.

"Do you know this Jude?" Riel questioned Reuba, thinking that avoiding the subject of the young man would be a waste of time. Everyone was interested.

"Yes, I saw him recently in the marketplace with his father and some other shepherds. He is a fine-looking son of Abraham!" Reuba flushed with excitement.

Neither girl was paying much attention to each other. They both strained their ears to hear the servants of Ben-Jared, but the announcement had abruptly ended since they were now lowering their pots to get water from the well.

As with many young, active minds, thoughts of the improbable, the unobtainable, the unusual, the impossible began forming in Riel. The morning dream of a handsome young man walking with her through a garden now had a name, Jude. It was not unusual for young servant girls to dream of the handsome prince carrying them away from their life, but Riel would have died from embarrassment if anyone could have read her thoughts.

Since her parents' death and her stepping into the life of a servant, Riel had seldom allowed herself to engage in frivolous dreams. She now chided herself for her indulgence. "Where do these thoughts come from?" she reasoned again as she had so many times. "I have nothing to give. No young Israelite would ever want me."

Riel struggled with the strength of the dream and its

The Women at the Well

power to lead her thoughts. "No, I think when I am a little older I will go to Jerusalem and give myself to the work of the Temple," she triumphed over the dream.

The declaration satisfied her for a matter of seconds and then vanished. The desire for love and companionship was too strong in her, and she could do little to control it. Riel hurried from the well as soon as she could, but the hope of love lingered in her heart.

For the next several days, her mind would quickly run to thoughts of this mysterious young male of Israel, the son of Ben-Jared, the wealthy shepherd. Though she would not admit it to herself, her trips to the well became information-gathering missions for news about this prince.

As could be expected when nothing comes to encourage the dreamer, she chided herself to resign to the fact that her future was bleak when it came to having a husband. "The servant said he would soon be betrothed. Why do I think of him? He belongs to another," Riel said over and over as she tried to thrust him from her thoughts.

Kira noticed that Riel was often at the loom, weaving and working with the wool from Broody. She did not appear to be in sorrow, so Kira did not question her. But the soft cloth that Riel was weaving to perfection grew longer and longer as the first cold winds of winter blew in Bethlehem.

6
Saagi

The weeks of autumn had passed and the shorter days of winter came, forcing Riel to spend almost all the sunlit hours carrying water. She did not want to be on the road after dark. The inn needed more water than ever because the flow of travelers had not stopped since the end of harvest. Everyone in Israel was answering the census of Caesar Augustus.

Riel was again watching the western skies on her final trip of the day from the well to the inn. The golden sphere of light sat on the gentle peaks as though waiting for someone's attention before it began its descent. Its brightness turned the distant hills black and accented their peaks and valleys.

She took a deep breath and started up the steepest of the three hills. She often made a game of climbing the hills. "I can make this hill in sixty-four steps; I know

The Swaddling Cloth

I can. Sixty-four! I can do it."

Her record was sixty-five steps, and if she were to beat the record she must do better. Her legs stretched as far as they could to accommodate her goal, but when she reached sixty-four there was still quite a space between her and the worn seat where she rested each day. "Who has stretched out the hills?" she mused with a laugh, realizing she was more tired than she realized.

Riel rewarded herself at the top by taking a rest in a small group of trees that grew close together at the edge of the small plateau, only a little distance from the road. It gave her a place to sit her pot down and to get her breath. An aged tree had fallen in front of the group of trees, giving the appearance of a stout fence protecting the younger trees. Riel sat on the fallen tree and leaned against the younger. It made a perfect resting chair. The bark was gone from the broken tree, and the timber had grown smooth and polished from tired travelers taking their rest. She carefully grasped the rough handles of the water pot and lifted it from her shoulder, placing it firmly on the ground beside her.

Israel was a land that the world walked through. The Egyptians from the south, the Syrians to the north, the nations to the east—they had all walked through Israel. The mighty Roman empire was now their captor and continually sent emissaries back and forth. Riel had a window to the world when she sat to observe the people walking Bethlehem's road.

Riel particularly liked the excitement brought by passing caravans. With their long lines of camels, men from faraway countries, and servants dressed in strange and exotic clothing, they were the provided choice entertainment for the Jewish people.

Just at that moment, Riel noticed a long row of camels coming toward her from the north. As she strained her eyes in excitement, she suddenly started. This caravan was different. It did not carry only trading goods from faraway places.

"Roman slave traders!" she gasped. From the looks of the camels and the number of water skins they carried, she could tell they had crossed the deserts of Arabia.

The slave traders were Romans who profited by crisscrossing the known world, kidnapping people, and selling them as slaves in faraway places. They were hated and feared and brought terror to every place they visited. Children and servants were most often their victims.

Riel slowly eased behind the fallen tree, hoping not to draw attention. She scooted to the end where the exposed roots made a perfect covering for her to see but not be seen.

Stories of the slave traders flashed through her mind: brokenhearted mothers whose children were never heard from again, servants who were not missed until they were miles away, and the cruel treatment the victims received in order to break their spirit. She could feel her heart beating wildly, and she placed her hand on her chest to slow it.

The caravan passed very close to Riel's hiding place. She was curiously excited, yet terrified, to be so close to these mysterious people of whom she had often heard tales of horror. The camels were loaded with treasures, some in sacks, some clearly seen such as ivory chests and golden furniture.

As Riel watched, she trembled. A group of young,

The Swaddling Cloth

strong men were walking in a cluster with chains around their ankles. Their shackles caused them to walk with staggered steps. She knew at once they were the choice youth from some village or city. Probably everyone else whom they knew had been slaughtered. Suddenly a smaller boy, no more than nine or ten years, fell. In an instant, one of the guards was upon him, flogging him fiercely. Riel gasped with horror.

"O God, have mercy on that boy," Riel whispered, knowing there was nothing she could do to help him.

Suddenly every muscle in her body tensed. Her water pot was still in view! What if the guard saw it? But the line of men, camels, and slaves kept moving. The moment seemed endless. Fear gripped Riel so tightly she could hardly breathe, and her whole body ached from the tension.

"The poor little boy, the poor little boy," she cried to herself over and over.

Just as the last camel was passing Riel's hiding place, a tiny bundle sitting atop it suddenly slid down the huge animal and hit the ground running. It was a child! In one movement the little one had jumped over the dead tree and landed only inches from where Riel sat watching the sequence in disbelief.

The child raised her head and looked Riel straight in the eye. Though covered in dirt, the child was easily identified as a girl, a frightened one. The older girl and younger girl, frozen in fear, stared into each other's eyes.

Riel could hear the sound of the caravan moving into the distance, yet she remained too frightened to move. She expected an eruption of confused sounds as the rough guards came looking for their tiny female possession, but no such noise came. Minutes passed as they

Saagi

both felt the same fear, listened for the same noises, and drew strength and courage from one another.

Riel slowly reached out her hand. The child was now shaking so violently, her teeth chattering. As Riel's hand touched the girl's shoulder, the brave little creature began weeping silently. Tears ran from her eyes but she made no sound. The older girl reached her other hand out and pulled the trembling child to her. She knew the kind of hurt that produced tears with no sound. The scent of fear permeated the child, and Riel recognized it. Stripes from a whip marked the child's face and neck. Riel held her close, and in those few minutes, the two bonded. Trust for each other was formed.

The reality of what had just happened slowly began to dawn on them. The younger girl realized her newfound freedom, and the older girl, her newfound responsibility.

"I will never give her back to them," Riel vowed in her heart. "No matter what!" The child did not belong to that caravan, and Riel had no intentions of running after it and offering her to those cruel and wicked men.

Once Riel purposed in her heart she would not force the child to return to the slave traders, she realized the two of them had to get back to the inn. Lifting the water pot, Riel pulled the child close and wrapped the loose end of her robe around her, hiding her in its folds. Riel kept their pace very slow because, in order to reach the inn, she had to walk in the same direction as the caravan. Neither said a word, but they both sensed the danger they were in.

I must reach the inn was the overwhelming thought in Riel's mind, but it did not keep other thoughts from coming. *What will Kira think? What will Nathaniel*

The Swaddling Cloth

do? What if Michal hates the child? I'm lucky to have a place to live, and now I am bringing home another mouth to feed!

While she had no idea what Nathaniel and Michal would do, she knew in her heart that Kira would welcome this little girl with open arms. Riel tried not to worry about her position at the inn, but her skin prickled in apprehension.

"Jehovah, help us," she prayed earnestly with every step.

When Riel saw the back trail that ran through the woods to the inn, she felt a glimmer of relief. She reached a hand down to the girl and patted her head. "We are almost home. Be patient," Riel tried to reassure, not knowing if the child understood her. No sound came from the child under the robe, but she kept pace with Riel.

At the edge of the clearing, Riel paused. "What do I do now?" she panicked.

"Kira will help us. She is a wise woman. She will know what to do," Riel declared rapidly, trying to calm herself and the small girl at her side.

"Any Israelite would help someone captured by Roman slave traders!" she finalized her decision, knowing that what she was doing was right.

There was no movement in the clearing of the inn, Riel noticed with perturbation. She glanced toward the stable to see if anyone was working there. Only the donkeys looked up from the stable door to see the misshaped Riel move toward the side door of the inn that opened into the food room.

Riel sat her pot outside the rough-hewn door. She

Saagi

paused for the briefest moment to consider the consequences of her next step. Would she find safety inside, or would she lose her place in the inn?

Riel quickly fumbled with her robe, opening the folds to reveal the child. The two girls stared at one another; then the child shivered, causing Riel to drop to her knees beside her. The child's eyes were large with fear, and yet something about her steady gaze hinted at her bravery. The bonding that had occurred at the broken tree held fast. She trusted Riel completely.

"I am going to take you inside to my friend, Kira. Don't be afraid. Don't be afraid! Do you understand?" Riel spoke slowly and child-like.

The child simply stared wide-eyed and remained silent.

Riel turned and pushed open the door, shutting it as soon as they were both safely inside. They stood motionless, waiting for their eyes to adjust to the dim light of the room.

Kira looked up from her kneading with delight. She loved all children and was pleased to see the small figure standing in the doorway. "Well," she chuckled as she squeezed the dough off her fingers one at a time, "who do we have here?"

"The men were so bad, and she fell, and I didn't know what else to do," Riel stuttered and stammered breathlessly, making no sense.

Kira made her way to the two girls and immediately knew the newcomer was not just one of the children of Bethlehem who had lost her way. "Peace and blessings be yours, my little one," Kira spoke with great kindness and tenderness, leaning down so that she might observe the child more closely.

The Swaddling Cloth

The child reached over to Riel and wrapped her tiny arms around the folds of her robe. Kira did not try to move toward the child, not wanting to frighten her with too much attention.

"Where did you find this little one? She does not look or dress like the children around here, does she?" Kira kept her voice low and kind.

It was the first time Riel had noticed the child's clothing. They were very unusual. Though covered in dirt, her clothes were of very fine cloth that had been sewn and designed in ways unlike anything the servants of Bethlehem had ever seen!

"Oh, Kira, you will not believe what I have just done!" exclaimed Riel as she pulled the small girl's arms from off her leg and reached down to pick her up. Words poured out like water from her water pots. "She fell from a Roman camel, Kira. It was a caravan from far away. She was terrified. I knew she did not belong to those wretched, cruel men. They beat their slaves unmercifully!" Riel spoke with emotion.

"There were other children, a little boy," Riel's voice broke. "But she ran to me. I couldn't make her go back! I just couldn't!" Riel was crying now from fatigue and fear.

The old woman straightened and looked from one girl to the other. "If she is of any value—and my guess is that she is—they will come looking for her."

Once again panic swept over Riel. "We will have to hide her," Riel spoke with deep conviction.

Kira continued, "We have to talk to Nathaniel. I believe he will have pity on her and let her live here if she will work." She crossed her arms, shaking her head in amazement. "Well, for now the most important thing is to get her something to eat."

Saagi

"Thank you! Oh, thank you, Kira. I knew you would make everything all right!" Riel exhaled with relief.

Sitting the little girl in a chair, Riel stepped back to look at her as Kira quickly spooned out warm soup into a small bowl.

"I would expect her to be four or five years, don't you think?" Kira knew she must speak slowly and softly, so as not to frighten the little thing.

"Yes, and at one time I think she was well tended," Riel mused.

They both expected her to devour the food, but she paused and looked toward the ceiling. For the first time they heard her voice. Strange words came pouring from the girl as she rocked back and forth. They were words, yet there was rhythm to them, almost like a song or a chant. It went on for several moments and stopped as sharply as it had begun. The child then looked from Riel to Kira as if she were waiting for something. She sat very straight. Her knees were spread and bent, her ankles crossed and her feet drawn under her thighs as she sat in the chair.

Riel coaxed her several times, "Eat, eat."

Finally the young one held her hands out and rubbed them as if she needed to wash.

Riel laughed and ran for the basin. She held it as the girl washed her hands. Then she held her hands dripping over the basin as if waiting for a towel. Now, Kira responded by bringing a cloth for her to dry on.

"Kira, look at that! She would not eat until she had washed." Riel was amazed.

"I have never seen a hungry child do that," Kira observed and then went back to her dough, knowing she could not leave it drying for long.

Riel waited until the youngster finished eating, then again knelt beside her. The fear had left the child's eyes and she appeared relaxed and almost eager, yet she had not smiled.

"What is your name?" Riel asked kindly and quietly.

"Name?"

She looked thoughtful, then replied slowly, "Name . . . Saagi."

Riel was delighted and glanced at Kira. "Saagi? Saagi. That is a lovely name."

Saagi looked straight into Riel's eyes as she cocked her head to the side. "Name?"

Riel clapped her hands in excitement. "Riel," she exclaimed, pointing to herself. "My name is Riel, and she is Kira," she said, pointing her finger toward the old cook.

"Who taught you to speak the tongue of Hebrews?" Riel touched her own mouth. "How do you talk like me?"

"Boy . . . slave . . . speak," Saagi said the words, but they had a strange sound to them.

Saagi was finished with the conversation. She unfolded her legs, slid to the floor, and moved to the fire with the demeanor of royalty. Kira and Riel looked at each other, raising their eyebrows. She was a peculiar little girl, but one could not help being drawn to her. They both decided at that moment that whatever they had to do to keep her, it would be worth the effort.

The night passed without event. Riel persuaded Saagi to remain behind the large barrels in the area where she and Kira slept, until they had finished serving the guests of the inn. Riel managed to drag one of the most worn mats from the sleeping areas for Saagi. Kira

Saagi

had spoken to Josiah and asked him to begin weaving a new mat of flax as soon as possible.

The nights were growing colder, and the woven clothes were brought from the rafters for the travelers to cover themselves. Kira found a small badger skin for Saagi. She seemed especially grateful for the covering.

All at once the child bolted for the door. In an instant she was outside with Riel stumbling after her. Riel swung open the door to race out and almost stumbled over Saagi. She sat with the same stillness that she possessed before eating. Only now she gazed upward. Her eyes went to and fro across the heavens. Riel was mystified but remained still. Something about Saagi's manner let Riel know that this was a sacred time for her. It would be her nightly pattern. Finally Saagi rose, made her way back to the mat, and was asleep in a moment's time.

"Kira, I am going to the marketplace in the morning to see if any of the slave traders have returned looking for our little friend," Riel spoke thoughtfully and bravely after she and Kira had laid their mats on either side of the sleeping girl.

"Riel, you must be very careful. The slave traders are evil men," Kira spoke gravely.

"There is no danger if I go alone," Riel reasoned. "I will be fine."

"I will pray," spoke the kind soul who knew the only One who could protect Riel.

That night, Riel dreamed she walked on the hills of Judea with the one she loved, only now they walked with Saagi between them. It was a night of rest and peace.

The next morning Riel had a difficult time convincing

The Swaddling Cloth

Saagi that she had to stay with Kira while she went to the marketplace in Bethlehem.

"No, Saagi," Riel shook her head emphatically as she tied her few pennies in a knot at the corner of her garment. "You cannot go with me."

Saagi's eyes pleaded and she clung to Riel's robe.

Riel opened the door, then knelt to the child's level and pointed toward the trail. "Bad men. Hurt Saagi," she explained.

Still the child would not release her grasp.

Riel thought for a moment and repeated, "Bad men, Saagi. Hurt you," and she began acting like someone with a whip.

Saagi's little face froze in fear. She dropped her arms in resignation. She now understood.

"Saagi . . . wait," the little girl quietly acquiesced as Riel made her way to Bethlehem with a basket swinging beside her.

The Marketplace Merchants

The marketplace was divided into different booths, with a merchant presiding over each one. A variety of foods were in baskets, some sitting on the ground while others rested on long pieces of wood. The smell of the fruits and vegetables was wonderful to Riel.

As Riel entered the market area, several of the merchants nodded and smiled. They had grown to love the young orphan girl who had turned into a beautiful young woman. She never brought complaints, only encouragement. She smiled back broadly.

She teasingly began, "Now, Abraham, I'm wanting to purchase figs, not nuggets of pearls! You know they are late summer figs. What is your best price today?"

With his arms resting on his broad stomach, Abraham grinned slyly. He loved bartering with Riel. "These figs are better than pearls. Their flavor is magnificent! The

The Swaddling Cloth

travelers at the inn won't leave once they taste these on your table. You will have their business for life!" he playfully exclaimed.

"Oh, Abraham," chided Riel, "we don't want the travelers for life. Heaven forbid! There is enough work at the inn for the entire Roman army. I will give you a mite for a bushel and nothing more."

She laughed but her gaze simultaneously swept the people around her, for she had not forgotten her purpose in being there. Most of them she knew, and none looked like a Roman slave trader. She did notice a group of young shepherds standing close to the open-air shops. She recognized them as shepherds by just a glance because their staff hooks curved far above their heads.

"I'll take your mite, but I want a smile with it, for that warms my soul," Abraham's tone went from teasing to somberness in his last word.

"You are very kind to me, my friend. God will reward such kindness," she also spoke sincerely, knowing she had received a bargain. She then paused. "Are there strangers about the marketplace today?" she asked innocently.

"Strangers? They are everywhere. Great for business. You know that, Riel. No one is hearing the tinkling of Caesar's coins like Nathaniel."

Riel pressed her lips tightly, realizing the stupidity of her question with the country traveling because of the census. *How can I possibly know if there is someone looking for Saagi?* she wondered anxiously, biting her lower lip. She gathered her basket and moved to another merchant.

She asked guardedly, "Caleb, did you see that harsh Roman who was here earlier? He was so cruel when he spoke." Riel was trying not to lie, and asking a question didn't seem like a lie to her.

"No, I've seen no Romans today. Does Nathaniel have you out looking for business?" he teased as he placed a vessel of olive oil in her basket.

"The inn doesn't need more business right now," she laughed with relief.

As she turned to take one last look around the area, she sensed that one of the shepherds had turned toward her when she laughed. Her eyes met the dark brown eyes of a young shepherd looking intently at her. She immediately dropped her eyes, raised her veil, and turned toward the road.

There was such intensity in the way he had looked at her. Riel was puzzled by it, yet it felt good to be noticed.

She then shook her head. "Riel, he is looking at someone else, not you, so don't think about it." However, she also knew the only person behind her was Caleb, and she doubted that the young shepherd was looking at him.

Though she tried to push it from her mind, the look in his eyes could not be forgotten.

Riel lingered at the last display of late summer fruit. She couldn't help herself; she had to look one more time. She set her basket down and casually looked at the selection though she was not really looking. Slowly she looked once again at the group of young shepherds.

They appeared to be in serious conversation. "Probably it's the Romans and their taxes. Is that all Israelites can talk about?" She was irritated and disappointed that no eyes followed her.

She knew the one who had looked toward her. He was partially turned toward the group, now making it possible

The Swaddling Cloth

to see the profile of his face. His garments were much richer and finer than the others, and his face was perfect. For several seconds she stood frozen, staring at the young shepherd.

The shopkeeper called out to her, "Is something wrong, Riel?"

"No, no," she nervously replied. "I–I–I was just thinking."

She longed to turn and to look one last time at the shepherds but was terrified to do so. She shook her hands sharply as she stood there, as though that would clear her thoughts. She wasn't in the marketplace to look at shepherds; she was looking for Roman slave traders!

Though Saagi's situation was extremely important to her, somehow her head was filled with thoughts of the unobtainable young man. He was exactly like the young man of her dreams. And he was a shepherd. Her heart raced with the happy thought.

"O Jehovah, if there was some way that I would once again live the shepherd's life!" she pleaded, knowing she was asking for the impossible.

Suddenly Riel's heart jumped to her throat. A strange sensation ran down her arms, making her fingers tingle. The young shepherd was moving toward her. When he spoke, his voice was gentle like the sound of brook, "I was just thinking about buying summer fruit for my mother. Would you know which is best? Sometimes the shopkeepers try to sell me fruit that is going bad instead of their best."

Riel had to laugh as she glanced back at the shopkeepers. Her hand instinctively went to the side of her face to hold her veil in place.

Though he was looking down as he spoke, when she

laughed, his head shot up and he looked directly into her eyes again. "My name is Jude, and I am a shepherd from the house of Ben-Jared," he blurted with intensity and urgency.

The pace of Riel's heart made her feel lightheaded, and she could not speak. His eyes held hers for a few seconds and then she looked away, her face flushed with excitement beneath her veil.

He paused and looked away but still directed his words to her, "Are you of the city or of the hills?"

"I was born in the hills, but when my parents died I began working in the city," Riel tried to keep her voice calm.

Jude said nothing for a moment. "Working?" he mused over that word, suddenly realizing she was a servant. Her demeanor did not reflect the bearing of a servant. Realizing his silence might embarrass the girl, he tried to show kindness.

"I like your laughter," he volunteered, trying not to show his surprise at her status of being a servant.

Riel turned and looked into his face in disbelief but quickly bowed her head. She was unaccustomed to such consideration from handsome young Israelite men.

"You are too kind," she whispered in a voice that captivated the young shepherd, and recklessness came over him.

"What is the best part of your work?" he asked, trying to understand what it was about her that made his heart swell inside him.

"Oh," responded Riel without lifting her face, "it is the hills. They sing to me, speak strength to me about Jehovah. I walk most of the day carrying water." She looked

The Swaddling Cloth

up with intense interest. "What do you like best about being a shepherd?"

Jude looked at his staff, ran his hand down the smooth wood, and paused. He often asked people about their work, but no one ever asked him about his. "I think it is being alone with the sheep at night, and you will probably think that I am lying, but I love to sit and watch the hills change from day to night. The hills don't move, but they change colors." He stopped and looked tenderly at Riel. "I, too, love the hills of Judea."

Their conversation was interrupted by the call of one from the group, "Jude, let us get back to the hills."

"I'm coming," he called to his companions as he turned back to Riel. "It has been good talking to you." And he was gone.

Riel stood very still, feeling a vitality she had never experienced before.

"He likes my laughter," her heart sang.

She grabbed her basket filled with figs but did not feel the weight. Habit alone moved her toward the inn. Her mind could focus on nothing except the continual replay of the nicest words ever spoken to her. She was almost home before she realized she had forgotten to look further for the slave traders.

∽ ∽ ∽

Jude walked north from Bethlehem to his father's camp. He was restless. The servant girl in the market had attracted his attention. The graceful manner in which she moved was beautiful to behold, and he felt a drawing in his heart toward her.

The Marketplace Merchants

But a servant? The beauty of her form fascinated him, but there was more to consider in a wife!

Her eyes—he loved the look of her eyes—bright, wise, and thoughtful. It was almost as though they responded to his. And her laughter! The sound of it still echoed in his head. It held such joy.

He shook his head and wondered at his own absurdity, "Jude, you think like a fool. The woman is probably married." Yet while he rebuked himself for his foolish thinking, he could not get his mind off the girl's glance.

Intermingled with those thoughts was the innkeeper's daughter, the girl who loved the lamb. She was his girl, the one who had brought endless delight to his thoughts throughout the summer days and nights. Her laughter in the valley with her lamb had warmed his heart like no one else had ever done.

Jude shook his head, knowing that a servant could never be his wife. "The innkeeper's daughter is not a servant, and she would fit into the life of a shepherd," he said to himself with determined assurance, drawing upon the feelings from the past months.

"She is definitely the best choice for a wife, I am certain," he suddenly spoke aloud. "Father and I must go to speak with the innkeeper before someone else claims her for his bride," he lowered his voice to a mutter.

Having parted from the others he left the beaten path and set off across the hills to a quiet stream where he often took his flock. During the early summer months when the waters ran heavily, Jude had gone there many times to pray, and he felt a longing to be there now. He made his way to a grove of ancient olive trees that grew nearby. There he fell to his knees.

The Swaddling Cloth

"O great and holy God, You who hold the destiny of every man in Your hand, guide my steps," Jude pleaded. The words poured from him in a way that was uncommon for youth. Somehow he knew there was a God who heard him, and he petitioned Him with a secure faith.

He poured out his longing to his God for over an hour. Not just a longing to have a wife, a longing common to young men, but a longing to find a wife who would be pleasing to God. Jude had seen enough homes even in Israel where the husband or wife did not care for the things of God, and it was a miserable union for both parties. He did not want that for his life. He desired a wife who would walk right beside him in his journey to be a man of faith like his forefathers, Abraham, Isaac, and Jacob.

Upon returning to the camp, he made his way to his father's private tent. His conversation at the marketplace with the servant girl haunted him. He wanted the companionship of a wife. Of that, he was sure. He knew he could never bring a servant girl to his father's tents to be his wife, but a girl of the tribe of Judah would be clearly acceptable.

As he threw back the flap of the tent, he saw that his father was stretched out and resting on the floor. Jude did not want to disturb him, but Ben-Jared raised his head at the sound. "Jude?"

"I am sorry, Father. I will not disturb your rest." Jude tried to leave.

"No, Jude, stay. I was just getting ready to go out to the pastures," the elder sat up and rubbed the sleep from his eyes. "One of the shepherds spotted a wolf, and I kept watch with him most of the night."

Jude slowly twisted the edge of his headpiece, then

The Marketplace Merchants

rubbed his hands together slowly. "I believe I have found a girl I would like to have for a wife," Jude blurted. He could hardly believe his own words.

Ben-Jared was equally surprised at his son's words. "That is good, son," he stammered slowly, wondering if it really was good. "Who is the girl, and is she of the tribe of Judah?"

"I have seen her day after day playing with a lamb, and I want her for a wife. She is the daughter of Nathaniel, the innkeeper," Jude hurried on. "I want you to speak to him as soon as possible. I am not certain of her lineage, but I have heard he is of the tribe of Judah."

Even as Jude was speaking, he wondered why he was suddenly in such a hurry.

"Next time we are in town I will talk with Nathaniel. He is often there in the late of day directing travelers to his inn," Ben-Jared raised himself from the floor as swiftly as any youth. He looked intently at his son. "Are you sure? Jude, I had planned to choose a wife for you."

"I am ready, Father," he firmly spoke. "I have seen her almost every day, and I know she loves the same things that I love."

Jude pushed the flap of the tent and was gone, leaving a puzzled yet understanding father.

Jude and Michal

8

The stable was her hiding place. The soft warm color of the hay, the smell of the grain, the sounds of the animals all flowed together as a harmonic symphony to the girl of the hills. The afternoon sun shone into the farthest corners of the cave and covered the place with a warm glow.

"Saagi, we can play with the animals here now that it is cold," Riel explained to the child as she gently lifted Broody from the sheepfold and sat him in the hay. He was almost too heavy for her to lift. Riel began brushing the lamb, hoping Saagi would take an interest. With the return of winter, her nightly romps in the meadow changed to long visits in the stable.

Riel leaned against the small manger that Josiah kept filled with hay as she watched her new little "sister" play with the lamb. The ox and ass were led from their stalls at

The Swaddling Cloth

morning and evening to eat from either side of the manger. Both animals in their respective stalls, lifting their heads to watch the girls, shuffled about so that they too might be noticed.

Riel watched the two little loves in her life play together. "See, Saagi! I knew Broody could speak your language." Riel laughed with delight to see Saagi's joy. The young child knelt, embracing Broody's neck and chattering in her own tongue. Saagi's language mystified Riel; she had never heard any to compare to it.

A shadow fell across the three at play as the rough-hewn gate swung open. Michal stood in the stable.

For a brief moment, Riel froze, then quickly jumped to her feet.

"What is that beggar doing in my stable?" Michal hissed scornfully, causing Saagi to immediately bury her head in Riel's robe. "It does not matter now. Put that useless, dumb animal away and get to the house, Riel. Father just sent word from the marketplace that important guests are on their way here, and the servants are to prepare the house and the best food."

Riel dropped her eyes meekly and replied, "Yes, Michal. I will go to the inn at once."

She placed her hand protectively on Saagi's shoulder and headed out of the stable with Broody following close behind.

Michal paused, and her gaze fell on the lamb.

"Josiah is to kill a fatted lamb, and that one will do just fine," Michal pointed triumphantly at Broody.

Riel stopped. Of all the nasty, cruel words that Michal had flung at Riel, none had ever cut so deeply. She wanted to leap at Michal. Rage filled Riel's eyes and horror swept over her. She would die before allowing Broody to become a meal for Bethlehem's inn!

Before Riel could unleash her fury, Josiah appeared suddenly in the stable.

"Did you hear me, Josiah? Father wants this lamb prepared for the evening meal," Michal pronounced the lamb's fate with a sneer.

"Yes," Josiah acknowledged. "Most definitely. I will do it at once."

Riel could not believe her ears. Josiah kill Broody? How unthinkable!

Josiah was lifting Broody in his arms, looking straight into Riel's face but away from Michal. "I will take care of everything." He spoke to Michal but his eyes addressed Riel.

"Good," declared Michal coldly. "I will inform Kira that the meat is being prepared and that you will bring it to the inn as quickly as possible."

Riel stood motionless except for her eyes, which nervously searched Josiah's face. The sparkle in his eye sent joy racing through her mind.

"Of course Josiah will take care of everything," she sighed with relief.

Michal huffed past her with an air of superiority.

As soon as Michal left, Riel rushed to Josiah and Broody and threw her arms around both of them.

"Oh, Josiah, thank you from the depths of my heart," she cried as Saagi looked on in bewilderment.

The old man rubbed the lamb's coat.

"Thank me for what? We have several lambs named Broody. I named them today," Josiah chuckled.

Saagi had dropped to her cross-legged position, staring

The Swaddling Cloth

after Michal with indignation. Riel hugged Broody once more and glanced down at the small girl. The disdain the child felt for Michal was apparent. Riel quickly dropped beside her. "Saagi, do not hate. Do you understand? To hate is wrong. Even when you feel right in doing it, it is wrong," Riel instructed, to herself as much as to the girl.

She felt hypocritical, but her words spoke truth. While she did not always have control of how she responded to Michal's cruel tongue, she knew hate was wrong. Seeing the ugliness of hate on the face of the child caused Riel to check herself.

Reaching out, she gathered Saagi in her arms tightly. "I love you, little one."

Josiah made preparations to roast a lamb from the flock, and Riel flew to the food room entrance and grabbed her water pot to run for the well. "It must be someone very important to kill a fatted lamb!" she mused.

"I must remember to have a basin at the door for the guests to wash their feet. Nathaniel likes that for the special ones."

Riel made the trip to the well as quickly as her strong, healthy limbs would carry her. Just as she reached the back path to the inn, Riel saw Nathaniel and his visitors approaching the front of the inn.

She had to hurry! Upon reaching the clearing at the back of the inn, she called to Josiah, "Quick! Could you help me?"

The aged shepherd quickly left his place where he was roasting the lamb and hurried to the young woman's side just as Riel reached the back door of the food room.

"Josiah, could you wash the feet of the guests?" she asked breathlessly, knowing the importance of the ges-

Jude and Michal

ture. "I think Nathaniel would want you to do it."

"Of course, I will," the older servant assured her. "You are wise to be so young, Riel. Nathaniel would want me there when his guests arrived."

Josiah hurriedly removed the blood-splattered apron he had used when dressing the meat. Riel handed the pot to him as he made his way to the front door of the inn to greet the special group.

Riel walked into the food room, shut the door, and fell against it.

"I made it, Kira," she whispered, still trying to catch her breath.

"You did, and I am proud of you," Kira spoke over her shoulder as she hurried with the preparations.

"What needs to be done?" Riel asked. She reached for the wine skins, knowing that Nathaniel would want the best wine for the guests he was bringing.

At that moment, they heard the group arrive. "I wonder who is causing all the fuss," Riel muttered out loud as she pulled the skins from the high shelf.

"It must be someone very important," replied Kira. "Nathaniel sent two boys from town to announce their arrival to us."

"No one is important enough to do what Michel wanted. Oh, Kira, you could never imagine her demands: to eat Broody for the evening meal!" Riel exclaimed in horror.

Kira shook her head, "Why does that girl, who has the best of everything, delight in destroying things that make no difference in her life?" Riel did not go into the main room to serve the guests because of her fear of Michal's wrath. As badly as she hated not helping Kira serve, she knew to stay away.

The Swaddling Cloth

She strained her ear to hear the conversations, but none could be distinquished except Nathaniel's. His voice was especially loud and jovial.

"What is Nathaniel so excited about?" mused Riel, knowing that the innkeeper's volume betrayed his regard for visitors. The more important the guest, the louder his voice.

As Kira returned from serving a large bowl of fruit, she matter-of-factly stated, "It is the wealthy shepherd I've heard about lately. Once just a simple man, his flocks have now grown beyond measure, and they are said to have the finest wool in all Israel. Ben-Jared is one of the family names of the tribe of Judah and their leader. Ben-Jared must be a very wise man."

Josiah pushed open the door from the main room and entered just as Kira spoke. He added, "And what robes they wear! I have never seen such fine wool. Even his son's robe is of the finest."

Riel froze. *O God in heaven! Could it be the young shepherd from the marketplace? He mentioned the Ben-Jared family.* Riel's mind was shouting but she made no sound. The wine skin slipped from her fingers and bounced across the floor of the food room. Josiah, Kira, and Riel all leaped for it.

"I am so sorry. Thanks be to God it did not burst," she whispered intently, knowing the value of the wine. She carefully scooped up the container and laid it on a tray.

He is here! The shepherd is here! Over and over rang the words in her mind, causing every fiber in her being to tingle. Riel's heart so filled with emotion she could hardly think. As Kira and Josiah stood together, looking at her, she was overcome with affectionate feelings for them. She rushed over and put her arms around both of them. "You both mean the whole world to me," her heart full of emotion burst forth into words.

The two old servants looked at each other and then at Riel, and the three of them laughed heartily. None of them knew why. Love flowed between the three that could not be explained. When Riel's heart overflowed from time to time, her two companions sensed it and enjoyed it as much as she did. They had no idea what had caused her happiness to overflow at that moment, but they felt it and were blessed by it.

Nathaniel's voice boomed from the main room, "Have you heard any news out of Rome, Ben-Jared?"

As the shepherd replied, in a much lower volume, Riel noticed something very familiar about his voice. She had heard that voice before. As a child at her father's fireside on the hills of Judea, with the sheep lowing in the background, she had heard that voice. She hurried to look out into the room.

"Kira, my father knew this man," Riel spoke in whispered earnestness.

Kira moved to the doorway. "Are you sure, Riel? You were so young, and your father probably knew lots of shepherds," she spoke with uneasiness.

"Oh, yes, I'm certain. His face looks familiar, too." She clasped her hands with excitement at the thought that she knew the father of the young shepherd! A sense of pride filled her to think that she personally knew the person of importance. Her eyes went cautiously back to the son.

Jude had knelt close to the fire and now threw back the head-piece of his robe. His dark hair was held in place by a band of wool wrapped around his forehead.

The Swaddling Cloth

Riel turned from the curtain and leaned against the wall separating the two rooms. Such feelings coursed through her body that she could hardly speak. Her arms had an aching tenderness in them.

Saagi suddenly appeared at her side, not saying a word but knowing something had come over Riel. Kira turned back to serving the food, not noticing Riel's reaction.

Riel knew she must remain calm or have to answer to Kira. For reasons Riel did not understand, she just couldn't share what overwhelmed her at that moment. Though she could hardly admit it to herself, Riel knew that what had suddenly come over her was love of the deepest sort. It was love so strong that it could last a lifetime.

The girl of the Judean hills gazed out the window at the clouds that were moving in. She prayed, "O God, why did my heart choose someone I can never have?" Two very strong emotions clashed within her. She longed for what she could never have. Riel fully knew she was not in a position to marry anyone of that stature.

"I wonder what Ben-Jared wishes to discuss with Nathaniel?" she pondered, pushing the warring feelings to the hidden places of her heart as she moved to help Kira load the food trays. The two men's voices were lower now, and with the other guests arriving she could not make out any more of their conversation. She longed to serve the guests so that she might go near them, but the thoughts of Michal unleashing her poisonous tongue on her in front of the shepherds kept Riel away. The thought of such humiliation in front of someone she cared for caused Riel to shiver. She could not tolerate the slightest chance of it happening.

"What is he doing here? How do they know Nathaniel?"

Jude and Michal

Riel's mind raced. *Life has such strange twists in it!*

Since she had seen Jude and spoken those few words to him in the marketplace, Riel had thought of little else. She knew the foolishness of what she had allowed her mind to do. Part of Riel's uneasiness now was due to the fact that she had allowed her imagination to run wild. She had dreamed of being Jude's wife, returning to her beloved hills, watching the sheep, having children, all the things that are reserved for young women on the verge of marriage.

She had created in her mind a rescuer, a deliverer, someone to free her from bondage, not of endless work but the bondage of insignificance that she lived with each day. From one conversation, Riel had made Jude the champion of her imagination; now she realized the futility of dreaming of romance with the unobtainable. The thoughts and dreams seemed harmless, but now that he was sitting in the next room, she knew it was a foolish fantasy. She scolded herself for being so silly.

All the while Riel was wrestling with those uncertainties, the knowledge that Ben-Jared had known her father caused another storm in her thoughts and imagination. She had a deep longing to know more about her family. She knew so little about them. When her parents died, it seemed a dark curtain separated her from her past. Thinking that someone might know of her kinsmen sent a wave of emotion through her.

Kira noticed it. "What is wrong, Riel? Why do you tremble so?"

Riel dropped her hands to her sides and twisted the sides of her robe self-consciously. She looked at Kira with a look of bewilderment that caused the older woman to

The Swaddling Cloth

laugh. "Dear little one, we have only to get the food out to the inn's guests, not decide how to conquer Rome," she teased.

Riel laughed, too, looking at the floor for a time and then raising her head with a smile. "You are right. I take things far too seriously, don't I, Kira? Why do I do that?"

"Because the touch of God is on you, and you feel things deeply, just like He does," explained Kira as she raised the tray Riel had just filled and headed for the door.

Riel quickly pulled back the dividing cloth and then once again gathered the courage to steal a look at the scene in the next room.

Michal was sitting a few feet from Nathaniel, smiling sweetly. The veil on Michal had dropped and it now cradled her face. She serenely looked about the room and shyly glanced at Jude before returning to the handwork she held in her lap.

Riel watched as Michal turned toward her father and Ben-Jared, and blushed because of some kind remark from the shepherd. Nathaniel was beaming like a full moon.

Riel watched as all this transpired, still unable to make sense of it.

Suddenly Jude rose with a look of determination on his face and went to where Michal was sitting. He stood for a minute and spoke with her, but she did not raise her head. He then lowered himself to sit on the floor beside her chair and spoke softly to her. When Michal raised her eyes and looked straight into Jude's eyes, Riel moved away from the door.

A sickness enveloped Riel. She grasped finally what her heart did not want to believe. Jude was there to choose a wife. Riel knew enough about shepherds to

Jude and Michal

know that they did nothing haphazardly. Caring for sheep left little time for meaningless socializing. No, the shepherds had a mission.

Disgust filled Riel but not at anyone other than herself. "What a fool I am!" she scolded with the fury that Michal usually unleashed on her. She flew about the food room cleaning, scrubbing, and putting things away.

Saagi sat in her usual manner, following Riel with her eyes. She knew something was wrong but had no idea what created the problem or how to fix it.

The hard work could not stop Riel's mind. She reprimanded herself over and over, "Why did I let myself dream of the unattainable? I knew he could never be interested in someone like me." She felt some type of comfort from her scolding, but it did nothing to take away the pain throbbing in her heart.

Finally, Riel gave voice to the deepest part of her pain, "Why did it have to be Michal?" Once the final blow was put into words, the tears came, making their embarrassing march down her cheeks. She had held back the disappointment while she scolded herself, but, alas, when she finally faced the fact that the one Riel chose to love had chosen Michal, her worst enemy, it crushed her spirit. The sorrow that she carefully managed to hold at arms' length all these years suddenly fell upon her in a deluge. The losses of her life crowded together, placing an unbearable weight upon Riel.

Riel quietly opened the door that led outside. Saagi jumped up and walked quickly to her. Riel closed the door and dropped beside the child with tears still running down her face. "No, it is too cold for you to be outside, little one. You stay inside. I will only be a few minutes."

The Swaddling Cloth

Instinctively, the child could feel the hurt that Riel was experiencing. She reached her thin, little arms around Riel's neck and hugged her tightly. Never was kindness more appreciated. It touched Riel and eased the wrenching pain of young love lost.

Saagi released her grip and backed away from Riel. Riel smiled at her and reached for the handle of the door. "Kira will be right back," she assured the child before stepping into the night air. The child unrolled her mat and lay down. Saagi sensed that her friend needed something that she could not give her.

Riel stood on the step, looked up at the grand sky with all its shimmering flecks of light, and remembered God. Her tears stopped and her faith returned.

"Forgive me, Jehovah. I had forgotten You," she put both her hands behind her neck and continued her gaze at the night sky. "My pride caused this disappointment, didn't it? I knew that Jude could never be mine. Please cleanse me from my selfish arrogance," she prayed softly. "I'm sorry for crying, too. Thank You for all Your goodness to me. You have blessed me in giving me this place, Kira, and Josiah, and now little Saagi. I am grateful for Your benefits and all that You have provided." The prayer was the most genuine in nature; prayed in faith, it touched the heart of God.

As her eyes scanned the heavens, feasting on its beauty, she noticed an unusually bright star in the eastern sky. *How did I miss seeing that before?* she wondered. She continued watching it, and it seemed as though it moved.

Riel squinted her eyes and watched it. "The heavens declare the glory of God," she quoted one of the psalms taught to her by her father. "I knew the stars moved in the night, but I did not know some moved more swiftly than others," she dismissed it with little thought.

After a while, she slipped back inside the food room and lit the old oil lamp. Riel hurried about cleaning and straightening the room. When Kira returned, all the work was finished.

"I believe this old tired body needs to make its way to the mat early tonight," she chuckled. "Riel, you have worked so hard, too. Let us rest."

"I will, Kira," replied Riel, "but first I would like to weave for a while."

Kira paused for a moment, thinking to herself, *What has caused my little one to want to weave after so much work today?* Kira knew that Riel would explain her troubles when ready; thus the old cook's thoughts quickly turned to prayer, the only way she knew how to help her young companion.

Riel sat at the loom and ran her fingers across the cloth. It was growing longer and into a perfect piece of wool cloth; soft, strong, and beautiful. She worked for several minutes, and with the flow of the loom came the calming of her emotions. She again went to her Lord and repented of her foolish thoughts, and little by little a warm comfort began to wrap itself around the brave young woman.

After an hour, Saagi rose from her mat and came to Riel, sitting on the floor beside the loom. "Oh, little honey," whispered Riel, "you must go to sleep."

"Sad. Riel sad," the little girl spoke quietly with a quiver in her voice.

Riel smiled, "No, I'm fine. Now go back to sleep."

"Saagi sad," she spoke softly. "Home. Saagi go home."

Riel stopped her weaving and pulled the child into her arms.

The Swaddling Cloth

"Where is home, Saagi?" she spoke aloud but scolded herself for her self-pity. The child's pain was so much greater than her own.

Saagi lifted her robe and pointed to her tiny leg above the ankle. There was a small circle with stars inside it, clustered on the far upper right side of the circle. Riel looked at it closely, turning the child's leg toward the light of the fire.

Saagi pointed at it again. "Home."

"Oh, little one. I'm so sorry. I wish I could help you. I have no idea where your home is." She moaned in grief for Saagi and held her tightly and prayed for her. When she finished, she gently stroked the child's head, knowing that they shared a loneliness that few people understood. She glanced at the child's ankle once again, wondering why she had not noticed the marking before. It was a perfect circle, and the stars were tiny and exact.

For several minutes, the two sat holding one another. Slowly Saagi reached out and touched the beautiful cloth that flowed from the loom, "Bad men stole Saagi. Saagi only looking at camels." Tears ran freely down both girls' cheeks.

"I'm so sorry, Saagi. Riel is sorry," she repeated over and over.

Kira lay on her mat in the corner and prayed for both of her little lambs. She softly spoke out, "Riel, I asked Nathaniel and he gave his permission for Saagi to live here if she will work hard."

"Now, Saagi, did you hear that? Things are starting to get better already," Riel said excitedly with a smile on her tear-streaked face.

She extinguished the lamp and carried Saagi to the middle mat.

Jude and Michal

Saagi reached up and kissed Riel's cheek, causing warmth to come to the older girl's heart.

"Peace and rest, Saagi . . . Kira. God is good, isn't He?" She spoke in the quiet darkness with only the glow of the dying fire.

"Yes, He is," returned Kira.

Michal rose early the next morning and pulled out her beloved mirror. She turned her head from side to side gazing upon herself in the polished brass. She touched her face lightly, running her fingers across her cheek.

"The young shepherd wants me for a wife," she mused seductively. "Silver, gold, jewels, garments! The time has come for me to take my place in the world, but it won't be among the sheep!"

Michal's head began to dance with visions of swirling silks, banquets, dignitaries, and men of renown seated at her feet. Few thoughts were on Jude, only on his wealth.

"I knew it would come! I deserve so much better than this foul sheep town."

While she wanted to spend time in thought concerning her future with the wealth of Ben-Jared's son, her eyes were drawn to her window where Riel walked in front of the stable. Romping at Riel's heels was a lamb with something around its neck. The color was purple and it had the same impact on Michal that the color of red has to a bull. She recognized that the lamb was Riel's beloved lamb, Broody.

"Josiah lied to me," her eyes narrowing with intense hatred. Nothing incensed her more than the lack of the

The Swaddling Cloth

servants' respect toward her. Revenge seethed inside her.

"They can't do that to me," declared the young tyrant. "I'll get that lamb. I dare those swine to disobey me!"

Michal was angry and she wanted out. She charged out the front door and stomped away from the inn. She wanted to run out and strike Riel, but she knew better than to risk marring her face in a fight. Riel was stronger than her. When Michal reached the main road, she stopped. A flock of sheep with their shepherd was headed north and they were using the main road to Bethlehem. She did not want to brush up against the animals so she remained aloof at the side of the road.

The young shepherd waved to Michal but she ignored him. He nonetheless paused, "I am headed to the Temple to take the lambs for the sacrifices. I work for Ben-Jared."

His proud boast longed to impress the young woman but she continued to ignore him. She stood at the edge of the road looking back at the inn, wanting so badly to hurt someone or something.

"These lambs would not be so calm if they knew the slaughter in store for them," he made a feeble attempt at humor hoping to draw the innkeeper's daughter into a conversation.

Suddenly Michal showed interest. "I have a lamb that needs to be sacrificed. He is a very unruly animal, constantly wandering. Would you take him to Jerusalem for me?" she queried sweetly.

"It would be my great pleasure." The simple shepherd assumed he was halfway to a betrothal.

Michal instructed him to wait and she made her way back to the stable. Riel was nowhere in sight. In a matter of minutes Michal located the lamb with the purple piece

Jude and Michal

of cloth woven about his neck and placed Broody into the care of the naive shepherd.

Michal returned to the inn with her back straight, her chin lifted haughtily. Revenge tasted sweet.

As the flock made its way closer to Jerusalem, another flock came into view. Jude was criss-crossing the hills looking for the last grass before the frost killed it.

"Shalom," called Jude to the younger shepherd, recognizing him.

He returned the greeting excitedly. Boasting to his master's son was an opportunity the younger shepherd rarely enjoyed. "I passed Bethlehem's inn and a beautiful maiden stopped me and asked me to take a lamb to the temple for her. I think she cares for me."

Jude knew the boy well and knew he lived in a world of dreams but he glanced in the direction that the boy pointed. Jude's face revealed his shock when he saw the purple sash about the lamb.

"Where did you say you got this lamb?" he questioned earnestly as he stepped over to the terrified little animal. One could easily see that the lamb was extremely well cared-for and groomed.

"The innkeeper's daughter placed him in my care and gave me two mites. She said the lamb roamed and needed to be sacrificed," the boy persisted.

Jude spoke firmly, "I will take this lamb. I am certain that there has been a mistake. I will give you a first-born lamb from my flock to offer in the Temple to replace this one."

The boy longed to protest but recognized the tone in Jude's voice. To argue would be futile. He shrugged his shoulders and yielded. "The girl would never know," he

The Swaddling Cloth

reasoned within himself and continued with his dreams.

As Jude watched the boy move his flock north, he reached down and picked up Broody. The lamb recognized the gentle touch of the seasoned shepherd and placed its head under Jude's strong arm for protection.

"I will care for you, my little one. You have nothing to fear," Jude rubbed the lamb's head and pondered what the boy shepherd had said. He touched the ribbon of purple wool about its neck.

This doesn't make sense, he thought in bewilderment. *There must be an explanation.* He moved his flock forward and pushed the incident aside for the moment.

Michal and Riel

A wind that grew colder each day blew across the hills, changing their color, altering their softness. Yet the hills remained immovable. Other cold winds had blown before. The hills survived the change.

Nathaniel announced that the house of Ben-Jared was returning for another visit: this time he would bring his wife. The inn would host an all-day feast in their honor. With all the family members of Ben-Jared plus the guests of the inn, it would be a crowded event. The three servants were faced with endless work.

Josiah prepared for the roasting of the meat while Riel and Kira gathered the ingredients to bake loaves and loaves of bread. Fruits and vegetables were obtained by trading goods with their neighbors. Wine skins were brought from the marketplace. Kira, Riel, and Saagi were pressed to find an empty spot for their sleeping mats,

The Swaddling Cloth

since the food room overflowed with supplies.

Saagi seemed puzzled by all their busyness. She would do the work assigned to her, but as soon as she finished, she drew her feet under herself, crossed her arms across her chest, and looked at the three with an air of royalty. Josiah, Kira, and Riel delighted in the little girl's manner. Riel learned to give the child little jobs that coincided with her own work, though she would not take the child to the well. Someone might notice the child and report Saagi's whereabouts to the Roman rulers.

Michal became more cheerful and cordial, causing Kira and Josiah to make several comments about her improved disposition. Riel listened to them with an ache in her heart. Michal's countenance reflected her happiness since Jude's visit.

Riel ceased dreaming of the young shepherd, but she felt safe in trying to remember more about Ben-Jared and his visit with her father. Knowing someone linked to her childhood made her former days seem more real to her.

The day before the feast, Riel and Saagi found a break in the work and made their way to the stable to spend time with the animals.

"Broody is probably very angry with us," Riel teased Saagi, and the child smiled.

Riel looked down at the child and shook her head. Wrapped in old wool for warmth, her feet in sandals much too large for her, yet she carried herself like a queen. Saagi's demeanor amazed Riel.

Saagi's eyes caught Riel's. Riel could sense enormous wisdom in those young eyes. When they reached the sheepfold, Riel's eyes searched for the purple cord

Michal and Riel

among the bundles of moving fluff. Broody was nowhere to be found.

She took Saagi's hand and sought out Josiah.

"Josiah, I can't find Broody," she nervously spoke, praying for an explanation.

"Oh, I am sure he is there. I'll help you look." He put the wood down and walked into the stable.

For several minutes they examined the fold to no avail. Broody had disappeared.

Josiah was perplexed. "Riel, I'm sure he returned last time we were out on the hills. I can't think where he would be. Surely he will turn up. Perhaps he wandered into another flock." Yet while Josiah spoke, he knew it wasn't possible.

Worry seized Riel.

"I will talk to every shepherd I know. With that streak of purple about his neck, he can't go far," the old shepherd tried to settle her fears.

I am so thankful that I placed that cord about his neck, she thought, trying to imagine Broody in a neighboring flock. She knew they could not begin the search for a while.

She put on a cheerful face, and together she and Saagi went to another part of the stable to play with the animals but her heart ached for the face of her favorite. What had happened to her little lamb?

∽ ∽ ∽

Riel was helping Kira remove a large vessel of pottage from the fire when she heard the guests' arrival to the inn on the day of the feast. There were many people entering the main room, and she heard the young voices of those who were now walking around the inn. Riel was excited and exasperated at the same time, yet she made every effort to appear only interested in the work that had to be done. The noise drifting into the food room told of happy, excited people.

"Well, how is the chief shepherd of the finest flocks in Israel?" boomed Nathaniel, whose eagerness to please amazed the servants. "There is no finer wool or meat in all of Israel than that from your flocks, my friend. We are honored to have you in our humble inn."

Kira and Riel looked at each other and laughed.

Kira whispered low, "He never mentions the inn's humility when he wants payment for a night's lodging." Riel nodded knowingly.

Ben-Jared's comments could not be heard, but Nathaniel's words grew louder than ever, "Yes, oh, yes. Michal especially loves the flocks. Sheep are her favorite of all the animals."

Riel's emotions had been especially stretched for several days, and when Nathaniel's comments reached Riel's ears, she began to laugh until she had to lean against the wall for support. Kira caught the merriment and, leaning over her kneaded dough and placing both hands on the table, she laughed until she shook all over though not making a sound.

Even Saagi, who was wiping out drinking vessels, joined the lighthearted moment. It was Saagi's loud laughter that forced the other two to control themselves, and both turned to the child, waving for her to stop.

The laughter sent a balm to Riel's soul. Suddenly, her entire outlook changed. Anyone who could be happy with

Michal and Riel

Michal could not possibly be right for Riel.

That viewpoint had not occurred to her in all of her musings of the last week. The truth comforted the young woman. She felt relaxed and confident in herself and God's ability to lead and guide her life. An amazing transformation came over her in those few minutes of laughter. Of course, God knew what she needed more than she did!

"Kira, I am going to help you with the serving. There are too many people for you to do it alone," she declared. "And," Riel smiled gratefully, "Michal seems to be in far better spirits lately."

Riel headed into the main room, carrying a large tray of fruit. Though her courage had taken a turn upward, she still avoided the area of the room where Jude, his mother, and Michal were quietly conversing.

Just as Riel and Kira carried in the last of the food for the feast, a knock came at the front door. Nathaniel kept talking as he made his way to the door.

Nathaniel welcomed the travelers with open arms. "Come in! Make yourselves comfortable. You are just in time for a great feast," he continued to boom.

He led the travelers to the sleeping rooms to store their belongings and to quietly extract the coins for the night's lodging. His voice always went soft when he discussed money.

Ben-Jared, left to himself for the moment, glanced at his wife and son and smiled. His eyes fell on the table, and he spied a dish that interested him. Riel continued unloading the tray.

Just as she stepped back to view her arrangement of the food, she collided with the shepherd, dropping the serving utensil she held.

The Swaddling Cloth

Riel reacted with horror and quickly bowed her head, "Please forgive my clumsiness, my lord."

"Forgive *me*, young woman. My eyes watched the food instead of where I walked," he laughed good-naturedly.

"No, no, I am at fault. Kira's food is so delicious, it is easy to forget everything around you," she stammered with her heart racing.

Ben-Jared laughed again. "Have you worked for Nathaniel long?" he asked with sincere interest.

Riel, swallowing her surprise at his interest, replied, "Yes, my lord, for seven years."

She nervously realized that Nathaniel would not approve of her conversing with his honored guest. She paused and dropped her eyes, weighing the costs of continuing the conversation. Ben-Jared stood close enough that she caught a gentle whiff of pastures, sheep, and an open fire.

Perhaps it was those scents bringing back nostalgic feelings of that most-loved period in her life. Perhaps it was the joy that the hard laughter had brought her several minutes earlier. Perhaps it was the renewed faith that she had just experienced. Whatever the reason, something caused her to throw caution to the wind.

She turned back to her work but spoke quickly, not looking up from the table, "My father, Ezra, was shepherd of the flocks of Judea. I believe you visited our fire late one night just before he and my mother died."

Just as she finished her last sentence, Nathaniel threw back the skins separating the rooms. His eyes focused on Riel speaking to his distinguished guest, and he exploded.

Michal and Riel

"Riel, have you gone mad? Get out of this place! We are entertaining important guests." His anger burned so fierce and his voice roared so loudly that every person in the room turned toward them. He shoved Riel away from the table.

She stumbled back falling but caught herself with an extended arm, feeling the rough wood of the floor digging into her hand. While his cruel words echoed in her head, she could still hear the silence that gripped the entire room. All eyes focused on Riel.

Michal jumped up and, in a voice louder than she intended, screamed, "Father, get rid of this daughter of Belial!" The hatred in her heart exploded from her lips. Jude and his mother's eyes dropped to the ground, embarrassed by the scene of anger.

Nathaniel spoke with a disgusted tone to Ben-Jared, trying to make amends for his rough behavior, "These ignorant half-breeds. Samaritan blood is all alike. They don't know their place. I should have never taken her in as a servant." Nathaniel laughed apologetically as he patted Ben-Jared's back over and over.

The innkeeper's voice continued and the other conversations in the room began again, but Riel's world came to a complete, dead stop.

She righted herself and rushed for the food room, Kira, and Saagi. As the animal skins slowly swung to their original position, Riel stood stunned and speechless in the shadowy food room, her heart frozen and her brain muddled. *Was he speaking of me? A half-breed? A Samaritan?* The scene, the words, the anger, and the scorn seared her mind. Jude and Ben-Jared's shock, the smug condescension of Michal after her outburst, the

The Swaddling Cloth

immediate silence of everyone in the room; all played over and over in her thoughts.

Gasping and sobbing, Riel stumbled toward the door to the outside and ran as far and as fast as she could. When she had run as far as she could into the hills behind the inn, Riel stopped. "A Samaritan? Me? No, I am an Israelite! I love the law. Jerusalem is the holy city." But while she stood shaking, a lone figure staring at the hills of Judea, slowly the truth dawned on her. Her mind continued its refusal, but in the deepest part of her heart, she somehow knew the truth.

Amazingly, so many things in her life began to make sense. Her mother's downcast eyes at the marketplace. Her parents' marriage and courtship were never mentioned in their tents. There were no wedding gifts sitting around as in other families. Riel remembered that her father never went to the synagogue. He loved Jehovah. He honored the Torah.

Now Riel understood. Father did not go to the synagogue because he was married to a Samaritan. He wasn't allowed in that holy place, nor was his wife or child.

The quiet disagreements between her parents about places of worship and the priesthood that Riel never had understood . . . now made sense. "No wonder no one stepped forward to take me when my parents died," she conceded. Like putting a broken jar back together, the pieces were falling into place. The completed piece spoke the truth. She was a half-breed; half of the Syrian race and half of the Jewish race. She had heard too many slurs about Samaritans not to know how people felt about them.

The dark shadow of insignificance swallowed her and bowed her to the cold ground. Hot tears streamed down her face while the rest of her being grew colder and colder.

After the fountain had quieted, she raised swollen eyes to her God. "I don't know what to say, Lord. This is too much for me to bear. I should never have been born." She tried to put together a prayer, but she was so uncertain of everything.

A familiar phrase in prayer came to her lips, "As my father, David, cried unto You. . . ."

She paused as her mind checked the words with the newfound knowledge. "Great Jehovah, *is* David still my father? Are You my God? This sorrow is more than I can bear." The pain of her loss engulfed her.

Two hours passed swiftly as she attempted to put her grief into words. Her belief of God's enduring mercy slowly ebbed back into her. Riel now spoke with her Lord on a deeper level. In the hour of despair, her God had not left her.

Quietness finally came over her. It was then, in the distance, she could hear Josiah calling her name. Knowing that he searched for her in the cold brought her to her feet. They were so numb she could barely walk; she stumbled her way to her precious old friend.

The relief of his face when he saw Riel touched her deeply. He gently placed his arm around her shoulders and led her back to the inn. No explanation was needed. His deep sympathy, as real as any beast of burden, helped carry Riel.

Kira had remained at the inn, waiting and watching for Josiah or Riel to return. The old Jewish mother had always planned to speak with Riel about her birth's circumstances, but there had never been a convenient time.

The Swaddling Cloth

"This would not have been such a blow for the girl if it had come from me," she chided herself over and over. Kira had wept bitterly as she had worked.

Little Saagi realized something terrible had happened though she did not understand. Together she and Kira sat by the fire after Ben-Jared and his household had left and the guests of the inn had turned in for the night.

"It is time to lay out the sleeping mats, little Saagi," Kira tried to sound cheerful. "You are usually asleep with the sun."

Saagi quietly unrolled her mat and then stood staring at Riel's mat.

"I do not know where she is," Kira answered with a broken voice, "and my worn-out legs would hardly get me to the stable." She walked over and hugged the small girl reassuringly.

Just then Kira heard the heavy, thick door slowly open, and she knew Riel had come home.

"Riel?" she whispered anxiously toward the opening door.

"Yes, Kira," Riel's voice betrayed the hours of crying.

"Thank you, Josiah, for looking for me," she wearily spoke and waved to the old man as he left her at the door.

"I'm so sorry, my precious one," Kira gushed in a broken voice.

Riel immediately crossed the room to the old cook's side. "Did you know, Kira? Did you know about my birth?"

"Yes, I knew," Kira admitted. "But I did not know . . . if you knew," she replied hoping that the young woman could understand.

Kira continued. "It did not matter to me, and I feared

Michal and Riel

mentioning it would make you think it made a difference. It was foolish of me not to make sure," Kira's voice broke again, and the anguish of her heart moved Riel. It was comforting to know that someone shared in her sorrow.

Kira poured out her deepest worry as she wrapped her arms around her. "I was afraid you wouldn't come back." She hung her head and her whole body shook.

Riel lifted her arms, embracing Kira, and the two comforted one another. Human touch can soothe the hurting soul.

"Kira, I know it is late, but could I weave for a little time? I cannot rest yet," Riel asked hopefully.

"Of course, child. I will get the oil and the lamp," Kira answered, so happy to be of some use to the young woman.

As she lay down, Kira could hear the quiet sobs. Kira was brokenhearted for her, but she knew that tears often form a river that leads to God. So she clasped her hands into a praying position and petitioned God to help in this painful situation. Kira understood the contempt that Jews had for Samaritans, and she knew the rejection that Riel was destined to carry for the rest of her life.

As the oil in the lamp burned, Riel continued to wrestle with her grief and pour her sorrow into the cloth. She worked the little strands of wool into the wooden teeth and pulled the shuttle back and forth, causing the long cloth to grow. And in her heart embarrassment wove its way into disappointment, disappointment into resignation. The simple innocence of ignorance was gone from Riel's life.

10
Ben-Jared

The night sky was clear and bright though there was no moon shining. The dark hills responded to the light by showing their gentle lines in the darkness.

On a hill of Judea, a lone shepherd sat on the ground by an open fire as late into the night as Riel. Ben-Jared had been greatly distressed by the scene that had taken place at the inn of Bethlehem. He and his family had left immediately, not touching the food of the feast. It was an insult to the host, but Ben-Jared cared not. The revelation of Nathaniel's words about the servant girl had been a blow to the man who appeared to have the world at his feet. As soon as the words of the young woman collided with the tirade of Nathaniel, Ben-Jared had a frightful realization quite different from Riel's.

The Swaddling Cloth

"Ezra," Ben-Jared breathed the words slowly, "my closest kinsman. . . ."

He placed his forehead on his crossed arms and leaned against his knees. "The poor child. She does not deserve to be a servant. Ezra would never forgive me for allowing it. His flocks became the inheritance that caused my wealth to increase."

He looked up at the hills that curved on and on into the darkness, "Jehovah, I did try to find the child after Ezra's death. You know I did." But the prayer rang hollow for the shepherd because, regardless of his effort, he had failed and now he faced the reality that a child of his own tribe worked as a servant in an inn with a cruel master.

As he wrestled with his mistakes and the consequences, he worked to devise a plan for Riel. "I will right the wrong. I must," Ben-Jared struggled. "But what if the girl refuses me? She has every right to hate the house of Ben-Jared."

He feared Riel's contempt when she learned that her father's flocks had been passed to Ben-Jared. And he, the receiver of Ezra's wealth, had not cared enough to search for the child left an orphan. Ben-Jared's shame weighed heavily upon him. As the great shepherd gazed at the hills and their abiding strength, he sensed a call to be courageous. A great determination came over Ben-Jared.

"Father?" a voice spoke outside the circle of firelight.

"Yes, Jude," Ben-Jared spoke but did not raise his now bowed head.

"It was an awful scene tonight, wasn't it, Father?" Jude spoke openly. Jude had wondered why his father had hardly said a word since it occurred.

Ben-Jared

"Yes, son. Far worse than you can realize," Ben-Jared spoke guardedly.

"Nathaniel and Michal are not what I supposed," Jude confessed.

Ben-Jared said nothing but thought, *How can I condemn Nathaniel? At least he has given the girl shelter and food.*

The young shepherd continued, "I spoke with Mother, and she is also afraid they are both not what they had appeared to be." He stooped to the ground and leaned his head forward against his crossed forearms, exactly like his father.

Jude continued speaking but mostly to himself, "It is remarkable that Michal is the same girl I saw in the valley who loved the little lamb. I misjudged her. She has a nature I could never live with."

He turned his head toward his father. "Forgive me for taking you and our family to the inn. I let my heart love someone who did not exist."

"No, son, do not ask for forgiveness. Jehovah wanted us to be there, I am sure," Ben-Jared spoke in a whisper.

They sat in silence for several minutes, each man reviewing the event from a different perspective.

"I will keep this watch for you. Sleep is far from me tonight," Jude offered.

"You are a son of whom I am proud, Jude. Why don't we take the second watch together?" Ben-Jared's voice was back to its normal strength. Together they walked across the hills toward the sleeping flocks, to relieve their herdsmen.

The Swaddling Cloth

Riel awoke the following morning before the dawn. As soon as consciousness came, there was a foreboding feeling, and then the awful memory barged into her mind. It took center stage again. The nightmare of Nathaniel's words repeated itself over and over until the young woman was in misery beyond description. It was hard to grasp the fact that one small statement, one chance encounter, could alter and taint all of life.

"Me, a Samaritan," she could not think of the words without feeling the hurt. "Why didn't someone tell me? How could I not know?" The question repeated itself over and over. She searched her childhood for clues. There were so many! It baffled Riel that she had missed their significance. To stop her thoughts, she arose. She had fallen asleep quickly the night before, but now sleep eluded her. Only an agonizing tiredness remained.

She did not dress herself as quickly as before. The sorrow she bore made every movement laborious, but she pressed on. Her position in the inn was in jeopardy, and Riel had to work harder than ever if she had any hope of keeping her place. But she felt no energy to do the work.

She wrapped herself in heavy shawls for protection from the cold morning air as she headed for the well, leaving Kira and Saagi sleeping. It remained dark outside, and the cold cut her like a heavy blow of an unseen hand. Her heart still ached so deeply that the cold wind went unnoticed, except against her swollen and feverish eyes. There the coldness felt good.

She held the pot in her arms. The burden she carried in her heart stooped her shoulders and bowed her head. A Samaritan. It was her only thought. Being busy could not stop her mind.

Ben-Jared

Riel arrived at the well and could not remember having walked there. She heard the gossipy chatter just in front of her as she stepped off the road to approach the well. She recognized the voices as some of those servants who would not speak to her. Now she knew why. She was a Samaritan.

"My mother told me with her own lips. He's decided on a maiden named Michal, the daughter of Nathaniel, who keeps the inn." Riel overheard it from a woman already at the well.

Tears blurred Riel's vision and she faced the truth that she already knew but had not spoken. "O God, it's true. Jude has chosen Michal," she sighed with a resignation of the deepest sort. "Michal is spiteful and mean. Surely such fortune would not come to her. Did not the wisest man who ever lived, King Solomon, declare that the wicked will not prosper?" she argued but then resigned herself. "Oh, what difference does it make?"

Riel wished it didn't matter to her, but it did.

As the conversation continued, the servants declared it was Jude, Ben-Jared's son, who had chosen Michal for his wife. Riel's heart ached and the pain pulsated in her arms and hands.

She left the well as quickly as possible and headed for the marketplace to buy lentil beans for Kira. Riel had heard her dear old friend say that she was out of the beans sometime that night before the ugly scene, when Riel's world collapsed. Riel's pain consumed her, yet she instinctively wanted to help Kira. She entered a stand and purchased the beans without incident and headed south toward the inn.

"Daughter of Ezra?" a voice called.

The Swaddling Cloth

Riel froze. She recognized Ben-Jared's voice. She would rather die than for him to see her again. She put her head down, and as fast as her feet could carry her, she flew from the marketplace. At the edge of town, she finally slowed her pace. The embarrassment, fright, shame, and physical exertion left her weak. She sat on a worn rock to rest. Her heart was pounding.

Ben-Jared had spoken without thinking when he saw Riel. He had been walking since dawn, thinking and pondering, trying to decide what to do. Now, seeing her fear of him, he was more unsettled than ever of what he should do concerning the girl.

"Perhaps I should just leave her alone," he lamented, not knowing if righting the wrong would only make more problems. "Surely the young woman would only hate me for my neglect," he struggled in contemplation. Yet seeing her in the marketplace confirmed that God wanted the shepherd to notice this girl who had suffered so much. A kinsman redeemer did not have a choice. He stood for a long time at the edge of the marketplace, looking over the hills, praying. He, too, felt no cold.

Returning to the inn with her head down, Riel entered the food room and heard guests quietly stirring in the sleeping rooms. The cold north wind blowing around the corners of the inn caused a hush over everyone.

Riel unwrapped herself and went to the fire. Embers were still glowing among the darkened cinders. She placed more wood on the fire and sat on Kira's stool, watching and waiting for the fire to begin to blaze again.

She stirred the embers with a long stick. *A Samaritan.* The words were branded into her thoughts.

"Where do I go from here?" Riel raised her eyebrows as high as she could, trying to keep back the tears. She had tried so hard to make the best of her life's situation. Becoming a servant had been hard, the persecution of Michal had been difficult, but as Riel focused on the good in her life, she was able to endure the hardships. When her parents died, she had been given Josiah and Kira. When Michal was unbearable, there had been Broody and now Saagi. When bad came, good followed.

Broody. Though she had hardly had time to think of it, she knew she must begin asking about Broody among the shepherds of Bethlehem. "Well, perhaps something really good is getting ready to happen," she smiled though her eyes glistened, missing the little lamb. "O Jehovah, please bring him back to me. I really need that little lamb right now."

At that moment, her eye caught sight of the cloth she had been weaving from Broody's wool. A beam of light streaking through the separating boards made the soft wool glow with warmth. She walked to the cloth, touching it with her cold hand, and brought it to her face. It felt so good to her. The strands of soft wool were perfectly woven together.

"I may be a Samaritan whom the people of my father despise, but I'm still an excellent weaver of wool and no one can take that away from me." The words started on a lighter tone, but by the end of her statement her throat closed and tears were coming.

She lifted the pot of water to begin her job of filling the basins. She dreaded going into the main room and

The Swaddling Cloth

having to face Nathaniel and Michal, but she knew the sooner she made the attempt to go back to normal, the better her chances of keeping the innkeeper happy. She quietly raised the skins that separated the two rooms and immediately began to work, but there was no sign of the innkeeper or his daughter. Where were they this early in the morning?

Michal was furious with her father. "Where are we going? It is just now the end of the fourth watch. Why are you dragging me out in the cold?" Michal talked to Nathaniel as she would scold her worst enemy.

Nathaniel said nothing and kept walking.

Michal stopped. "I refuse to go another step until you tell me where we are going. If I wanted to follow a lunatic, I would go to the tombs. Is that where you are taking me? Are we moving to the tombs? You are a lunatic, Father. I will give agreement to that, but I am not going another step. I'm chilled to death."

Her voice had risen steadily in volume, intensity, and cruelty. Nathaniel finally stopped and turned to her.

"Perhaps you did not notice last night, but something happened. I offended the richest man in Bethlehem. He openly insulted me by leaving, and if we are to continue living after Augustus's census, we will have to move the inn." Nathaniel now screamed as well.

He continued, "I don't know what we did, I don't know what I said, I cannot figure it out, but there is no hope for a betrothal between you and the house of Ben-Jared. I will take part of the responsibility, but your outburst didn't help."

Ben-Jared

"My outburst? I merely spoke the truth. I put an arrogant servant in her place. Anyone would agree with me," Michal retorted.

"You didn't see Ben-Jared's face. Listen, daughter." Nathaniel had returned to a more determined calm, sensing that he had said too much. "We are leaving Bethlehem and moving to Jerusalem. There are more rich men there; there are many people from about the empire traveling there. It is the place I should have started years ago."

He placed his hand on her shoulder, but Michal jerked away. "Michal, I have here many, many gold pieces." Nathaniel pulled back his robe and revealed a great leather bag that extended across his back and under both his arms. "I have enough wealth to buy you anything you could ever want. We will start a new life in Jerusalem. But I have to purchase the land today. I wanted to wait until a new season, but I cannot put it off any longer. We will purchase the land, bury the remaining gold on the land, and return to the inn tonight before more guests come. We must work quickly. I wanted you to see it before I purchased it."

Seeing the leather bag filled with gold coins softened Michal.

"Father," she cooed sweetly, "You have done well. Why didn't you tell me?"

Nathaniel felt a wave of relief that she had responded so quickly. "Daughter, here's something for you to keep," he exclaimed. Looking both ways to make sure no eyes saw him, he slipped two pieces out and put them in her hand.

"Father, we are rich. Yes, we have it all! Who needs the house of Ben-Jared? And let's get all new servants!"

The Swaddling Cloth

she laughed low and gleefully.

"Yes," he joined in the laughter, glad that the storm was over.

Now the two turned toward Jerusalem side by side. Nathaniel would make the purchase and still be back before travelers began filling the inn.

11
Mary and Joseph

As the afternoon drew to a close, the number of travelers at the inn swelled rapidly. Josiah, Kira, and Riel worked diligently to make everyone comfortable. Josiah washed the guests' feet, Riel refilled basin after basin for cleansing, and Kira, with little Saagi's help, prepared the food for the evening meal. It would have to be pottage tonight with so many to serve.

When Nathaniel and Michal returned at dusk, the inn was filled to capacity. Guests would be sleeping in the main room, but neither Nathaniel nor Michal seemed concerned.

Riel and Kira worked tirelessly bringing in the food. Many of the travelers had to sit on the floor, but most seemed happy to have a place to rest, sleep, and eat. With the inn filled with happy, chattering, paying strangers, the disaster from the night before appeared forgotten, much to the relief of the servants. The innkeeper's voice

The Swaddling Cloth

could be heard above the clamor.

Later, as the mats were being distributed and every inch of the inn filled, a steady, quiet knock could be heard at the inn's door. It was pointed out to Nathaniel by a traveler placing his mat close to the entrance. The innkeeper made his way to the door but only opened it a small crack because of the cold air. It was largely unnoticed, but there were a few remarks made, money exchanged, but no guests entered the inn.

Only later Saagi came into the food room to announce to Kira, Josiah, and Riel that people were staying in the stable.

"On this cold night?" exclaimed Kira to herself. "What will Nathaniel do next to satisfy his greed?"

Josiah slowly raised himself from the warm, food room fire and began wrapping his heavy robe about himself. "I will go to see what the child is speaking about. Kira, put some pottage back on the fire in case there are people staying in the stable and Nathaniel has forgotten to offer them food," he spoke with quiet concern as he made his way out the back door.

Kira moved her tired body toward the pot that held the remains of the pottage.

"Let me help you raise that to the fire," Riel stepped over to her.

When their hands were on the handle, Kira looked at Riel. "It is good to be busy. God is good to give us lots of work this night." Her sweet, kind face watched Riel hopefully.

"It is good to have work," replied the weary girl, knowing what Kira had meant. The cook had worried all day how they would return to normal after last night.

Mary and Joseph

As they lifted the pot to the hook above the burning wood, Kira said with satisfaction, "I think everything will be fine, and we can go back to living as before."

The back door suddenly opened, flew back, and hit the wall. Josiah hurriedly reached and pulled the door back to its closed position. "Kira, it is much too cold for you to be out, but the people whom Nathaniel has put in the stable without fire or food are a couple from Nazareth—they have come so far," he paused to catch his breath. "A young married couple, and she is about to deliver a child," he finished in a hushed tone with his old eyes wide with shock.

"What did you say?" asked Kira, quickly making her way to Josiah. "She is delivering a child in the stable?"

"Yes, and it is their first. They seem as surprised by it as I am," he spoke in a shocked whisper as he handed Kira her heaviest robe hanging by the door.

Just then there was a gentle knock. Kira already had her hand on the latch. She lifted the latch to see a young man with a very humble demeanor standing outside. His hands were in tight fists at his side, and while he seemed somewhat calm, his voice shook with emotion as he spoke.

"My name is Joseph of the tribe of Judah. I am a carpenter now living in Galilee, but I am here for the Roman census. Would you come to help my wife? Her time of travail has come, and I know nothing by which to help her. We are not afraid. God will help us." His torrent of words fell on sympathetic ears.

"Yes, of course, God will help your wife, and so will we. I am Kira and have helped many young mothers bring their young into this world. There is no place here in the inn to bring forth a child." She looked at the crowded

The Swaddling Cloth

food room and knew every part of the inn was crowded, brimming with people or supplies.

As Kira wrapped her cloak around her, she turned to Riel, "Empty the rag barrel into a sack, quickly. I will need them all. I must go to the young woman. Oh, yes, get all the oil lamps we have and our heaviest skins. She and the child will need warmth.

"Riel, if I need you, I will send Josiah, but for now, rest. I'm sure the young mother will need help in the morning." With that the old cook was out the door, holding an old lamp.

The glow of the fire threw shadows about the room as Riel rushed to get the things Kira had requested. Joseph stood waiting. He took the lamps and sack gratefully and made his way back to the stable.

Josiah knelt by the fire with Riel and Saagi. It felt as though a storm had just blown from the room.

"I hope they are all right," Riel spoke the sentiments and the helpless feeling of all three.

The old man thoughtfully rubbed his short beard as he watched the embers. Josiah spoke slowly with great disgust, "Nathaniel's greed has turned him into an ox, and the only person on this earth more vile than Nathaniel is Caesar Augustus for demanding that all of Israel move around the countryside like a herd of cattle. A daughter of Israel having a child in a stable, it is unthinkable!" Seldom did the old servant speak so harshly.

The inn was quiet, more so than usual. The three sat silently by the fire. Saagi was leaning heavily against Riel, fighting sleep. Slowly, the room began to have a warm glow of white light coming through the cracks and crevices about the room.

Mary and Joseph

Riel noticed it first. "Josiah, look how light it has become in here. There is no bright moon tonight."

Josiah replied, "I wonder if it could be that star that I have watched for several nights? It seemed as though it was moving from the east. In all my years, I have never seen a star like that. Well, perhaps the light will help Kira bring the new babe into the world. God is good."

The Christ Child

The old man, the young woman, and the sleeping child sat in front of the quiet fire, waiting for the news of the newborn. Riel's troubles were forgotten in that time of concern for the young family.

Just as Josiah rose to add more wood to the fire, the back door opened, and Kira returned. "She bore the child alone," she said softly, looking at them. "By the time I returned to the stable, Mary, the young woman, had bore the child, her first-born son." Kira removed her robe, held it in her arms, and leaned against the closed door.

Josiah and Riel waited patiently for her to continue.

Kira turned and washed her hands in the basin by the door. "It was the most unusual experience. Such a peace dwelt in that place, even warmth on this cold night. The animals. . . . Oh, Josiah, you have never seen the animals behave in such a manner!"

The Swaddling Cloth

She shook her head and slowly dried her hands on the cloth tied at her waist. "But that is nothing compared to the child! Oh, the child, the child is like an angel! The expression on his face and the solemn look in his eyes, I have never seen such a child. Surely God is in that place."

Kira looked at them with wonder. "I know you probably won't believe me, but even in that dark cave, I did not need the lamps. There was light."

Kira pulled her stool to the fire and sat warming herself. Kira looked thoughtful for a moment and then turned toward the weaving structure in the corner of the room. "Riel, would you see your way to give the child the cloth you wove from Broody's wool?"

Riel's eyes followed Kira's. She had finished it only last night. It represented many trials in her life and reminded her of the little lost lamb. The long, soft cloth folded neatly on the stool caught the star's beams and seemed almost to glow in the dark. No hesitation came. Riel loved the soft blanket, and even if she had not felt enormous compassion for the young family, she could never refuse Kira.

"Of course, Kira. Take it to the child. It the best I have, and the baby should have it."

Kira reached over to Riel and patted her shoulder, "Thank you, little one." She paused. "The young woman in the stable is very much like you."

Riel smiled, but sadness stole across her face as she said in her heart, *No, she is not like me. I am an outcast in Israel.* But she said nothing. Somehow she had to push forward, away from all that had happened, but she felt helpless to go on.

Kira slowly stood and breathed deeply, "Riel, Saagi

The Christ Child

should go to her mat and you, as well. I will return soon, but do not wait for me. I must take the soft cloth to the child. The stable is warm but the night is cold."

"Yes, I must rest, also," said Josiah as he rose to go to the men's sleeping room. "I hope Nathaniel has not given my mat to a traveling camel." He spoke in jest but would not have been surprised to be without it.

The three moved in different directions, and as Kira opened the door, a glow of light entered the room. "Isn't this brightness amazing? I have never seen the night so bright," she exclaimed in a whisper and quietly made her way out of the inn to the stable.

Riel put the tired little girl on her mat and covered her with the last fur skin left in the food room. Saagi, whose eyes were already closed in sleep, reached her small hand out from the covers and patted Riel's arm.

Riel shook her head and smiled. Saagi was a strange child. At times her actions seemed regal. Her mannerisms were so unlike any child in Bethlehem.

She laid two woolen cloths on Kira's mat and then looked at her own. "I'll just sleep in my heavy robe tonight," she said, knowing there were no coverings left.

She lay with her face to the mat and pulled her legs under her for warmth. It also was her position of prayer at night before she went to sleep. "O God, You know every Israelite by name. Please help the people in the stable," she prayed in silence.

It felt good to Riel to petition God on behalf of someone else. Since the previous night, self-pity had overwhelmed her, and her thoughts had been filled with nothing but help for herself.

The pain remained. The shock of being something

that she never imagined would always stay with her. However, she was determined not to let self-pity remain in her heart. A true faith in God has no room for such pity. Faith declares that there is a God in heaven watching out for His own, and nothing can change that.

She lay there thinking of all that had transpired in her life. She remained troubled about the family in the stable. Where was Broody? Sleep eluded her.

Though her eyes were closed, she began to see the glow of light. She looked around the room and could not believe the brightness. The light was coming through the cracks of the walls.

"Surely it is not that star! It must be sunrise . . . but it couldn't be. I just laid down." Riel glanced around the room and saw the fire still burning.

She rose from her mat and shivered from head to toe, yet she had to find out about the illumination. Riel was surprised that the others in the inn were not awakened. The heavy snoring could be heard throughout the rooms.

Slowly and quietly, Riel lifted the latch of the door and stepped outside. The infinite sky could be seen in the distance, but there was a radiance lighting the heavens. She looked up in wonder. What could it be?

The light hung high in the sky, yet the glow seemed very near. Riel stared in awe. "A miracle is happening. Surely God is near!" She didn't know if she should fall on her face or run and hide. She watched the bright star and felt an aura of reverence.

As she walked toward the stable, the sound of singing drifted across the clearing. A thousand voices blended in perfect harmony. Riel stopped. The strains of melody seemed far in the distance, yet their beauty engulfed her.

The Christ Child

Reaching the stable, she heard the excited conversation of men coming from the valley below. She peered into "her" valley and was puzzled to see several men moving. "They're shepherds," she whispered to herself when she saw the staffs rising above their heads as they walked into the light of the star. Riel felt a sense of relief as she saw them walk toward the stable. She trusted shepherds.

Dropping behind a stack of wood, she waited to see what they wanted. The six shepherds paused as they reached the entrance of the stable close to where Riel was hiding. "How strange a place for our Messiah to be born," one man spoke.

Riel's heart fluttered when she heard it. It was Ben-Jared. The events that were taking place could not completely erase her previous encounter with Ben-Jared. His voice brought pain, but what he had spoken now was thrilling . . . Messiah? Here?

The shepherds quietly made their way up to the sheepfold and into the stable, leaving Riel outside. She paused, now afraid to enter, yet knowing it was the one place she could be free to enter.

Kira, Riel thought suddenly, gaining the courage to go inside, knowing her old friend was helping the young couple there.

She crept beside the sheepfold and then slid between the rough boards to get closer. When she reached the rocky edge that jutted out from the cave, she could see the shepherds. They were on their faces, giving obeisance. The men were worshiping God!

A strange and wonderful dawning came upon her—this place was hallowed ground. She edged her way along the cold sides of the cave to get closer. The glow of the

The Swaddling Cloth

star outside the cave gave a golden brilliance to the humble animals' dwelling. The loose-strewn hay caught the reflection of the light and created a carpet fit for a palace.

She drew near the herdsmen, but an ox stood blocking her view. It lowed softly as she ran her hand down the side of its neck. Riel felt almost at home in the stable and as the animals milled about they moved her forward. Riel's hands trembled with the cold, but her heart burned. Although the unpleasant feelings of the past few days lingered, she sensed that somehow she belonged to whatever was happening tonight. Her heart was afraid, but there pulsated in her body a new boldness that she had never experienced.

As the ox lowered its head, Riel saw the child lying in a manger. The majesty of the babe startled her. Never had she seen a king, but she instinctively knew now she was looking at the tiny face of a monarch. Riel slowly and reverently made her way to where the sheep were lying. Each one she passed looked up in gentle motion to receive the girl they knew. No intruder moved among them; this young servant was their own.

The shepherds seemed not to notice Riel, nor she them. All eyes were tear-filled and focused on the small infant. Lying on hay covered by the skins from the inn, Mary, the young mother, raised up and spoke to Riel, "Are you Kira's young friend who wove the swaddling cloth?"

Shyness, and then incredible joy, swept over the young servant girl. Her precious cloth enfolded the tiny child! The shepherds had called Him Messiah! A star shone over the place where He was born! The depth of the experience seemed unfathomable.

She wiped the tears from her eyes to get a clear view. Yes, her little lost Broody's wool, the cloth into which she

The Christ Child

had poured her sorrow to God, lay gently about the child. He must have heard her to allow such a miracle to happen in her life.

"Yes, I wove the cloth . . . from the wool of a lamb from this flock . . . and I am so honored that you would use it," spoke Riel in quiet and serious tones.

"Would you like to hold the baby?" Mary asked kindly.

Riel, filled with such joy, could not speak, but her eyes answered the young mother. Joseph, her husband, leaned down and lifted the child from the manger. Riel moved closer and reached out her arms to Him. Kira stood to the side, watching the scene with amazement.

"What is His name?" Riel breathed reverently as she looked into the child's bright eyes.

"His name . . . His name . . . is Jesus," said Mary as she lay back on the hay.

Riel patted the soft wool cloth as she held the child close to her. His little eyes drew her. They looked up at her so intently yet had such gentleness in them. What tremendous peace and love Riel felt! Earthly words failed to describe it. She knew beyond a shadow of doubt that God loved her! She knew it.

A transformation took place in Riel's heart. The horrible inferiority left her, and a great understanding moved into her being. She was changed. She had held the baby only for a few minutes, but a life-changing experience had happened to her.

"Thank you for letting me hold Him," she whispered to Joseph as she handed Jesus to him. Riel leaned down to Mary and said, "He is the Messiah, isn't He?"

Mary's young eyes glistened with tears as she nodded her head.

The Swaddling Cloth

Riel paused, glancing around the stable, and for some unknown reason spoke to the young mother the deepest things of her heart. "I recently learned that I am a Samaritan." She stopped and looked bravely into Mary's eyes, then lowered her voice even more. "I realize I am an outcast of Israel, yet God knows my heart and my love for Him. God allowed me to be here, the night of all nights. I know that."

Mary raised herself a little more and touched Riel's hand. "Jesus will always have a special place in His heart for Samaritans."

The two young women reached for one another's embrace as Kira looked on from the shadows, thanking God for the peace she saw on both their faces.

Riel was overcome with a desire to worship. She stepped back to the sheep and bowed her knees in prayer. She then leaned her face to the ground. She felt the prickly straw against her cheeks, but she hardly noticed it. She wept tears of joy like none she had never known. She glorified God. She wasn't insignificant. She was meant to be. God wasn't concerned with her bloodline. He cared and understood her just as she was.

After several minutes of praise to God, she raised herself and looked around, realizing the peculiarity of these circumstances. Here were grown men weeping and animals lowing, side by side, and in their midst was a newborn baby lying in a manger. It was all so strange, yet all who were there realized it was the most blessed place that had ever existed in the history of man.

Conversations ceased, but the murmur of quiet prayer could be heard. Riel felt absolute happiness, yet she could not stop the tears. She watched as each shep-

The Christ Child

herd bowed at the manger before the child. The Messiah had come to the world, and His birth was attended by all whom Riel held dear to her heart. God had chosen to make His entrance into the world among common men.

The child lay wrapped in His "robe," the swaddling cloth made by Riel's own hand. He rested in the midst of hay harvested from the fields of the earth. The manger, His tiny throne, Josiah had built. His attendants were the men of the flocks. And they were all gathered in a tiny cave on the side of a hill, a place where the inn's animals stayed.

Outside, angelic hosts filled the heavens with song, and a star shone brightly in the sky. Such a mix of the common and the miraculous!

As Riel thought about the weaving of the cloth, she reached down and patted the soft ears of a sheep kneeling beside her. "Wouldn't Broody have been proud?" she whispered to the animal.

When the cramping in her legs got her attention, she shifted her weight as the feeling returned to her limbs in sharp pain. She reached out and petted each of the sheep that had drawn around her, while she kept her eyes on the child.

Finally, she rose to leave the young family to rest. The hour grew late. The shepherds were beginning slowly to make their way outside. Only one remained. He, too, was silently weeping before the awesome scene. As he sensed the others were leaving, he lifted his head. Jude!

The young shepherd had reached a marvelous understanding during that hour in the presence of the Prince of Peace. God would direct his steps. He did not have to wrench from the Holy One the way he should go. No. God, the Great Shepherd, would lead. Jude knew he was loved by God. Jehovah had allowed him to see the greatest

The Swaddling Cloth

event in all of history . . . the coming of the Messiah.

Riel and Jude's eyes met, but Riel quickly bowed her head when she recognized him. She approached Mary and Joseph and said, "My life will never be the same after this night. I pray you can rest."

Mary nodded with understanding.

Riel retraced her steps under the ox's head and against the side of the cave.

Seeing Jude had brought those embarrassing feelings to her heart again, but somehow it didn't hurt. He didn't know she existed, but Someone else did and that mattered most to her now. Even if Jude never acknowledged that she was alive, they had shared in the greatest event in all of Israel's history. That would always bring warmth to her heart.

She heard the shepherds still conversing outside the stable, so she stayed at the edge of the sheep's fold, waiting for them to leave. She no longer felt the same shame and despair, but she did not want to intrude upon them. The sound of their voices began to trail off, and she knew she could walk to the inn unnoticed.

When she started across the clearing, a voice spoke softly from the darkness, "I am a servant of Ben-Jared and Jude, the tribe of Judah. You are the girl who loves the lambs, are you not? Ezra, the shepherd's daughter?"

Riel stood still, "Yes," she stammered, "but how do you know my father?"

She turned toward the voice, and then her eyes fell on another miracle, Broody. "Broody?" she whispered with sheer joy. The little lamb pulled at the cord, trying to get to Riel. She swiftly went to the animal and threw her arms around his neck. "I am so happy to find you! Where have you been? I have worried and worried about you, and you have been out visiting," she laughed and cried at the same time.

"My master must speak with you," the servant said earnestly. "He wants to ask permission to have your hand in marriage for his son."

"Ben-Jared?" she asked in shocked disbelief but immediately understood the mistake.

"Oh, no. You have asked the wrong girl," she replied softly. "It is Michal, the innkeeper's daughter, you have come to speak with." She thrust her face into the soft wool of Broody's coat.

"You are the girl who loves the lambs, are you not?" the man asked.

"Yes, but . . ." Riel tried to tell him his master had visited the inn to meet Michal.

He continued to shake his head from side to side, waiting for her to finish.

Finally, she shrugged with a smile, "You have the wrong girl. There is no possible way that it is me."

"You are the girl who knelt with the lambs in the stable tonight before the Savior, are you not? And does not this lamb belong to you?" he persisted.

Riel had stood and said, "Thank you for returning my lamb to me. I will repay you. Somehow I will repay you for your kindness."

"Then you are the girl my young master, Jude, wishes to marry," he pronounced firmly, ignoring Riel's words. "Would you consent to the marriage, and to whom must I speak concerning the marriage?"

Riel could hardly speak. "Kind servant of the house of Ben-Jared, it is not me, I am certain. If you knew the circumstances of my birth, you probably would not talk to me," she finished slowly, squeezing the lamb.

Before the aged servant could answer, out of the shadows stepped Ben-Jared. He walked up and stood behind Riel. Ben-Jared spoke gently, "Riel, I knew your father and mother."

Riel did not move. She remained with her back toward him. "Yes, my lord. I remember you at my father's fire," she answered.

"He was almost my brother," his voice broke with emotion.

Riel turned with shock and disbelief and looked straight into his eyes, "Your brother? My father was almost your brother? How can that be?"

Ben-Jared's hand went to his mouth and his fingers rubbed his lips as he tried to get words to come.

"Our fathers were of the same tribe of Israel, Judah, and we both were the only sons in our families. We grew up together and shared everything." Ben-Jared now looked at the ground.

He continued, "When he married your mother, our tribe disowned him, but I loved your father. He was a fine man. And your mother was an excellent woman." Now his eyes would not meet Riel's.

"By the time we heard of your parents' death, you had disappeared. I did not know what had happened to you until two nights ago at Nathaniel's inn." He glanced at Riel and then dropped his eyes again. "I should have searched for you, but with the growth of my herds, I waited and put off my responsibilities and let you slip from my grasp."

His voice became extremely earnest. "I made up my

The Christ Child

mind earlier tonight, while sitting on the hillside, that I would come to you and explain. And then there appeared a heavenly host singing and praising God! An angel instructed all of us who were on the night watch to come to this place. We were amazed when the angel said the Messiah would be lying in a manger . . . and then to discover it was the stable of Nathaniel's inn! I found the Christ child and you at the same place. God works in mysterious ways. You and miracles are wrapped up together, my young friend!"

Riel could not answer the chief shepherd.

"And tonight, in the midst of the miracle of the Messiah, my only son, Jude, realized he had made a mistake. It was not Michal, Nathaniel's daughter, who played with a lamb in the valley, but it was you, Riel. It is you who stole his heart out on the hillside," he ended with a smile coming to his face.

"Oh, . . . my lord! I have no words. Jude wants me? Your son?" Riel could not make sense of the things she heard.

"Yes, my son, Jude, desires you, Riel, for his wife," slowly replied the man with a smile.

Riel brought her hands to her face. Excitement, fear, joy, sorrow, every emotion she possessed, she felt. "I am not worthy of such honor. I have nothing to give. I am a servant . . . and a Samaritan," Riel tried to explain.

"Hush, young woman. I and my son know more about you than you do," Ben-Jared chided her yet with tenderness in his voice. "I will return when the work is finished. And, of course, I will redeem you from Nathaniel, whatever the cost. I am your kinsman redeemer. I will pay the price."

Riel felt astonishment; she knew a kinsman redeemer

was the hope of every orphaned child. "How could this be?" She had known such despair and hopelessness about her situation in life, and now to have it wiped away with a few spoken words. . . !

Riel began slowly, "If Jude is sure that it is me, Riel, a Samaritan, the daughter of Ezra, then I consent to . . . speak with him." She ended with a shy smile.

Ben-Jared and his servant bowed low, turned, and were gone, leaving Riel in the clearing alone. From the shadows, stepped Jude.

"Riel?" the young shepherd was timid, and his words were hesitant.

"Yes?" Her voice was as soft as the wind that blew around them. Riel remained kneeling beside Broody with her arms around his neck and her head bowed.

Jude walked around her and also knelt. Broody, recognizing the young shepherd, pulled away from Riel and rested his head on the arm of Jude. Riel's eyes widened with surprise. Jude must have cared for the lamb these last days.

When Jude bowed near, Riel detected the scent of the hills, and it filled her with comfort and happiness. She loved it.

"I have so much to say that I don't know where to begin." He paused, looking up at the star, then at the stable, and then back at the young woman.

"Many months ago, while out on the hills tending my father's flocks, I saw a girl. She was unlike any others. This person did not simply walk over the land; she was part of the land, coming and going across the hills at evening. Her play with the lamb intrigued me. She loved the things I loved. This shepherdess did not just care for

The Christ Child

the sheep; she loved the flocks. I could feel it from afar. I did not know where she came from, but watching her, I sensed she would be part of my future."

Riel smiled at this and lightly touched Broody.

"That girl would sit by the brook some evenings in prayer, and though afar off, I knew she loved the God that I loved. She would sometimes sing of her love for Him, and I could catch the melody on the wind. It brought such a peace to my soul."

He paused, looking at her bowed head, and then spoke more earnestly. "I loved that girl. With every day that passed, my love grew. Every time she ran down a hill with that lamb, my love increased. An unusual love, yes, because I did not really know her, but it was a real love that God allowed me to have. I knew Michal, Nathaniel's daughter, lived in the inn, and . . ."

Riel shuddered and lowered her head further.

Jude saw the shudder, reached out, and gently touched her shoulder. "I'm sorry, deeply sorry. I know now what a cruel person she is. But the girl," he hesitated, "the woman I loved . . . was you, Riel. I am here, in the glow of this marvelous night, to declare my love to you, to my father, to my God, and to anyone else who wants to hear!"

He then reached out with his hand and raised Riel's face that he might see her eyes. "I should have known in the marketplace that you were the one. Your eyes have the gentleness and stability of the hills, and I should have known then." He shook his head and looked down, dropping his hand. Jude stopped talking and waited.

"But my birth . . . my mother. . . ." Riel could not let that be ignored.

139

The Swaddling Cloth

"What? What about your birth? A Samaritan? What is that to me? What is that tonight, the night of all nights? Together we have seen the hope of all Israel and of the world! We are just lowly shepherds, some servants, and a Samaritan. I can't explain why God would honor us in such a way, but He has. If there was ever a moment in all of history when mankind is equal, it is tonight. Riel, I promise you, I love what you are. Salvation has come to Israel, and we are a part of it. God has brought us together, and if you will have me, we will marry and you will never be without a family again. You will never again be a slave to any man."

They both raised their heads at the same time, and Riel looked into the dark eyes of her shepherd, there in the glow of the star, and simply said, "I will be your wife."

Jude, looking just as deeply into her eyes, first smiled, then quietly laughed, and then he reached over and hugged the lamb. "I will first make us a home, and then I will come back for you. Be ready to go, and I will come for you. I don't know how long it will take me, but just be ready. My father will settle things with Nathaniel."

Riel laughed, too. "I promise I will be ready."

At that, the young man rose and moved toward the valley behind the stable.

There in the golden light of the bright star outside the stable, a young orphan girl stood in utter amazement at the tender mercies of God. With little Broody at her heels, she walked back to the outer edge of the stable and laid her hands on the walls of the cave.

For an hour, she praised God. Not in pious words that some would categorize as praise, but with every fiber in her being stretched to their highest level. Laughter filled her

The Christ Child

mouth and her soul. Joy pulsated in her being with every beat of her heart. Heaven noticed the kind of praise that broke from her soul. In the midst of all her sorrow of the last few days, she never thought she would ever know joy again. Yet, as she realized the miracle that God had given her, the understanding turned to incredible joy and the joy transformed itself into praise. The star in the heaven twinkled down at her as if it shared in her happiness.

"Messiah, the miracle of Your birth is covering the earth," she exclaimed, turning and running for the inn.

13

Kings of the East

"Saagi! Saagi, wake up. Something has just happened! No, a thousand miracles have just happened! I want you to see." Riel gently shook Saagi.

The child stirred and muttered but did not respond.

"Please, Saagi, wake up. It is the most wonderful sight I have ever seen, and there are so many things to tell you," she pleaded.

Saagi opened her sleepy eyes and looked at Riel but made no effort to rise from her mat. "Saagi tired," she moaned and tried to turn over.

"No," Riel replied gently but firmly. "It is a miracle, and you must see it. Now! Up!" she commanded as she pulled on the young girl's arm.

"Saagi will come," she sleepily answered while Riel began slipping her sandals onto her small feet.

With the younger leaning upon the older, they opened

The Swaddling Cloth

the back door to the clearing. The chill of the night along with the star's bright light drove the vestiges of sleep from the child. As they stepped outside, a different kind of sound met them, coming from across the clearing.

Riel's eyes turned toward the noise, and there at the stable stood several camels. They were huge beasts, and the light of the star made them look even larger.

Riel froze. "The slave traders!" She grabbed Saagi to thrust her back into the house. Riel knelt and put her arms around the child. Saagi was trembling uncontrollably.

"Save me. Saagi not go," she whispered in terror.

Riel prayed over and over, "God, help us." She knew they could not run. There must be a hiding place! Images of the Christ child, Jude, the star, the stable, all faded from her mind.

How could they be here on this night of miracles? *They've seen the star.* The child. Had the slave traders come to steal the holy babe? The overwhelming fear made it hard for Riel to think.

"Kira," she whispered but knew that her trusted friend remained in the stable, helping the young mother.

"Saagi, listen to me," Riel words were stern. "I am going to hide you in one of the huge water pots. I have to get help. Do you understand?"

The child threw her arms around Riel's neck. Riel rose to her feet, holding Saagi in her arms, and quickly stole to the largest water pot standing against the outside wall.

Just then, someone threw back the skins that separated them from the main room. It was Michal.

"What are you doing? Do I hear camels?" Michal demanded, not expecting Riel to answer her. "What are you doing with that bundle of filthy rags?"

Riel slowly lifted Saagi over the top of the clay vessel and lowered her into it without turning to look at Michal. She then walked to the child's mat and retrieved her coverings. As she pushed them into the darkness of the pot, she whispered encouraging words to the child.

Michal screeched yet in a whisper, "What are you doing, you imbecile?"

Suddenly Riel's fear and anger erupted in words as harsh as she had ever spoken. "Michal, silence your mouth. Do not say another word. We are in grave danger, and we all could die if you do not stop."

Michal was stunned into silence at the rebuke.

Riel continued, never taking her eyes off the darkened hole that now held Saagi, "Get out of this room."

At that instant, the outside door opened, and there stood Kira. Riel patted the pot and walked straight to Kira. Michal's eyes flashed, her mouth opened, ready to unleash a tirade, but somehow the good sense that was deeply buried in her took over and she turned and quietly left.

Kira tried to slow the quick intakes of air, "Riel . . . the camels . . . it's amazing." She tried to speak though her heart raced.

Riel interrupted with urgency, "I have seen them. Are they the slave traders looking for Saagi? What if they take the new child? What should we do, Kira?"

Kira's breathing slowed somewhat, but she still gasped for breath between words, "No slave traders, no." She swallowed hard. "They are kings, royalty, or something. I have never seen garments like theirs," she shook her head in astonishment. "I tried to ask their servants when I walked out of the stable, but . . . they speak another language."

The Swaddling Cloth

"Thank God, thank God. I thought those evil men had found out I took Saagi." Riel leaned against the side of the room. Her shoulders sagged.

"But I am not finished. What I had to tell you is . . . the language of the servants. . . ." The old cook could hardly speak, "It sounded a little like . . . Saagi when she gets excited." Kira finished in a loud whisper of fervor.

Riel raised her head, her shoulders, and her hands and looked at Kira with wide-eyed wonder. "Do you think the people on the camels are Saagi's people?" She spoke in shock and awe.

Kira shrugged her shoulders in a quick movement, "How do I ask? They do not understand me; I do not understand them. But wouldn't that be something?"

Riel was on her toes. "Kira, this has been a night of miracles!"

Kira's old shoulders shook with glee, and then she laughed aloud, "Yes, I know."

Riel jumped and ran toward the tall jar of clay. "Saagi's in the water pot," she threw her thrilled whisper back at Kira.

"Saagi, Saagi, come here to Riel," calming her voice, knowing the girl's fear. Though the child could not always understand the words, she quickly understood the tone. The gentle words reached into the darkness.

Riel pulled the stool to the clay vessel and braced her arms against the sides of the cold, hardened clay. The sides of the pot were cold to Riel's arms as she reached in.

"Saagi, Saagi, I'm here," Riel continued calmly. At first, she could not reach her. Then a small hand bumped hers, and with Kira's help, they pulled the cold and trembling child out of her prison of cold clay to freedom.

The child clung to Riel and would not let go. The stirring of the camels could still be heard.

Kira spoke again, "I will return to the servants and try to make them understand."

"No, Kira, you stay here with Saagi. Let me go to see if I can talk with them." The events of the past hour gave Riel new courage. Riel gently explained to Saagi that she had to go outside.

Once again Riel made her way into the stable where the holy child lay. It was still aglow with the light and warmth of the star, but a different group of people was assembled in the tiny "palace" of the new king. These men were of wealth and honor.

Even the servants wore garments like nothing Riel had ever seen. They all appeared to be royalty, yet they were all on their knees, bowing in obeisance. Riel waited and watched, loving every moment she was able to be near the child. She knew the hour must be in the third watch, but she felt no desire for sleep.

When one of the leaders closest to the manger reached out to place a gift of gold before the child, Riel felt her heart surge within her. A gold piece on the royal sleeve had carved into it a circle filled with black stars; the same figure she had seen on Saagi's leg!

Riel forgot about trying to talk to the servants. She calmly but quickly backed out of the stable, not wanting to disturb the worshipers, but then ran for the inn. Inside she grabbed Saagi from the mat where she and Kira were sitting in front of the fire.

"Oh, Kira, I think these people are Saagi's people!" she exclaimed breathlessly. She threw a covering over the child and made for the stable with Kira at her heels.

They stood just inside the cave, waiting for the

entourage to leave the stable. When the men stood to leave, Riel moved outside to where the camels were standing. As the group came into the open air, Riel could hear their muffled, strange language. With Saagi's head buried under the skins against Riel's beating heart, the child could not hear the voices until they were very close.

Suddenly her little head bobbed out of the waves of covers. Her fear dissipated and her eyes darted around. She had heard their voices! When her eyes fell on the first of the servants moving toward them, she cried out in indescribable joy. One of the leaders broke through the group in response to her cry. "Saagi?" he whispered as loud as he could with utter disbelief.

"Saagi!" He spoke the name again with gladness only a parent who has lost his child can express. It came from the deepest cavern of his soul, intense and longing.

Riel could not contain the little ball of excitement she held. The small body hit the ground, running right into the arms of the man whose look of joy, surprise, and happiness could not be described.

Father and daughter embraced and wept for a time without speaking a word.

"Saagi, Saagi, Saagi," he muttered again and again. The other kings and the servants of the group had fallen to their knees and were in a state of worship at this joyous, unexpected reunion.

Then Saagi regained her tongue, and the foreign chatter erupted from the child. Kira and Riel looked at each other, tears of joy streaming down their smiling faces. When the child finally paused, her father turned toward Riel and Kira. He walked to where they stood and fell to his face before them while Saagi stood.

"My father happy!" she exclaimed, somehow sensing that the two servant women felt uncomfortable receiving such an honor. "He gives thanks to you and to God. He has found the King of kings, and he has found Saagi. Saagi lost but Saagi found."

The king stood, reaching for Saagi, and began speaking in perfect Hebrew. He told of his bloodline in Persia and that, many centuries before, a young woman named Esther had come there from the nation of Judah. She had married one of his forefathers and had introduced to the royal family the worship of one God, Jehovah. As queen, Esther instructed the wise men that a day would come when a virgin would conceive a son and that He would be God with us, that a star would come out of Jacob and a scepter out of Israel. Since the days of Esther, they had studied the stars, watching for the one to appear to lead them to Emmanuel.

"We have loved the one, true God, Jehovah, all our lives, and tonight we have seen Him face to face," the king concluded as he looked back toward the stable. Father and daughter then made their way back into the stable, for he wanted her to see the great miracle that had taken place before they left to go back to the East.

Upon their return, he and Saagi exchanged words, and he turned to his servants and gave orders. The huge, dark men quickly disconnected a wooden barrel from the side of one of the camels and proceeded to fill it with untold riches. With each item, Saagi spoke: "For clothing Saagi," she said reverently as the servants placed rolls of cloth of unmatched beauty and texture inside the barrel.

"Oh, no!" Riel exclaimed. "You owe me nothing."

The child held up her hand as a signal for Riel to be

The Swaddling Cloth

silent. That ability to rule had not subsided throughout her ordeal.

"For warming Saagi," she explained as the servants placed rare and beautiful animal furs on top of the cloth.

"For feeding Saagi," several small bags of rare and precious spices were placed inside.

"For loving Saagi," shyly the child looked up at Riel as a beautiful box of fragrant scents was added to the gifts.

"For saving Saagi from evil men," she said with a broken voice as the servants brought bags filled with jewels and gold coins, more than Riel had ever seen.

As Riel and Kira stood in wonder and disbelief, the servants were commanded to place a lid on the barrel. Saagi then took a servant inside the inn and immediately returned with a burning log from the fire. Candles were lit and hot wax was put around the lid, sealing it. Saagi then instructed Riel to write her name in the hot wax. Riel did, with hesitation. She did not want to take the treasures but knew it would insult Saagi's father if she refused.

Riel lowered her head and spoke to Saagi, "Dear little one, I cannot take this wealth. It is I who should give you gifts. We did not know your father was a king."

The child reached over and went into Riel's arms, placing her small hand under Riel's chin and raising the older girl's face to look her straight in the eye. "Riel always my friend. Saagi must go to homeland." Her words were firm, and Riel suddenly realized she would never see her little friend again. Kira stepped over to her two little charges, and the three clung to each other in perfect love and devotion outside the dwelling of the Prince of Peace, in the light of a shining star.

Riel and Jude

A gentle wind blew across the everlasting hills of Judea. Only a week had passed since the miraculous night, and in some ways life remained the same at Bethlehem's place for travelers. Riel still carried rivers of water and worked as hard as any man in Judah, but the world revolved a different way. She told Kira some of the details of Jude's declaration of marriage, but it had been such an amazing event that she could scarcely believe it to be true herself. It was hard to share with anyone the words that were forever hidden in her heart. Kira's happiness burned as brightly as Riel's, but they both were somewhat bewildered by all that had happened. Not knowing what else to do, they fell back into their routine.

"Kira, I'll be in the stable," Riel sang out as she stuck her head in the doorway of the food room, leaving her

The Swaddling Cloth

pot of water after her first trip to the well. "I want to see baby Jesus once more before they leave."

Kira turned from stirring the fire to acknowledge Riel, but the young bird flew from the nest. Kira chuckled to herself, "Oh, to move that quickly!" She paused and looked down toward the fire. "What joy that girl has brought to me!"

She pulled her little stool closer and slowly tucked it under her to rest her short, weary legs. The events of the last several days had left the old servant overwhelmed yet happy beyond words.

The family in the stable had been Kira's primary duty since the night of the wondrous birth, though Nathaniel knew nothing of it. Nathaniel had tried several times to make them leave, but Kira had stood firm. The young mother needed her rest before taking another journey. Only yesterday, Joseph had expressed their desire to leave.

Because of his brutishness, Kira had never told Nathaniel of the miracles that happened that night. She longed to tell him and believed it only right to do so, but he would not give her a moment's audience. He had learned of Mary's giving birth, and he only wanted the young couple to be on their way. He feared Kira would soon have them in the inn, taking up valuable space, and he would not allow that to happen. Therefore, he would allow no conversation.

Kira walked to the doorway of the main room and lifted the skins. Nathaniel sat on the floor in front of the fire, staring. Kira entered the room quietly and walked to the fire. Michal was nowhere in sight.

"Nathaniel, I wish to speak," she started again.

Riel and Jude

"I'm selling this parcel of land. Michal and I are leaving, and we are moving the inn to Jerusalem. You will have to find other work." Nathaniel spoke with no feeling or emotion, only flat, lifeless words.

Kira was astonished. "We are leaving the inn?"

"No, the innkeeper and his daughter are leaving, not you," he spoke hatefully, and suddenly anger clouded his face. He grabbed a stick leaning against the wall and began roughly jabbing at the logs on the fire.

Kira stood behind him not speaking, just waiting.

Nathaniel's agitation increased. The confrontation with Riel in front of Ben-Jared loomed in his mind, aggravating and irritating him. Something in the chief shepherd's demeanor had changed at that moment, and he blamed everyone but himself.

"You idiot servants have ruined Michal's chances of marriage with the house of Ben-Jared, so we are leaving. Nobody is going to look down his nose at us, especially some sheep-stinking shepherds," the anger poured from him as he stood to his feet and turned toward Kira.

"And I want that family of swine out of my stable immediately. There is a buyer coming to look over the land, and I want that stable cleaned out." His rage continued, and Kira knew the best thing to do was to move away quietly and she did. Nathaniel himself turned abruptly toward the door to leave, and they parted without another word.

The innkeeper and his daughter never knew they missed out on the miracle of the ages. It did not have to be so. They chose to ignore all the paths that would have led them to the wondrous events. The miraculous was all around them, yet they were blinded by their

The Swaddling Cloth

selfishness, greed, and hatred. God came only to those who were looking for Him.

Kira returned to the food room and, once alone, sighed quietly with a deep feeling of calm, knowing that God continued to work on the behalf of the servants of Bethlehem's inn. Only a few days ago, such an announcement would have terrified the aging cook. However, the knowledge of a barrel covered in rags at the back of the food room completely settled her fears about the future. A smile stole across her face.

Riel reached the stable and respectfully called out, "Mary? Mary...?"

"Yes, Riel, come in. You can hold Jesus for me, if you'd like. Joseph and I are packing our things. Joseph just took the beast of burden to the well to drink his fill before the journey," Mary responded with a warm smile. The bond of friendship had grown, beginning with what they had shared on that night of miracles.

"The days of my purification are over, and now we must go to Jerusalem to present Jesus at the Temple. There we will offer a sacrifice." Mary spoke very tenderly, knowing that the subject of the Temple embarrassed Riel.

"I imagine it will cause quite a stir when you enter," Riel returned bravely.

"We will see. We will see." Mary pulled the treasures of the kings out of the hay and pushed them into an empty grain sack.

Riel gently raised the baby from the manger. Seeing the precious baby wrapped tightly in the swaddling cloth

Riel and Jude

thrilled Riel. She looked into His tiny eyes and felt love in every fiber of her being.

"Oh, Mary, I don't want you to leave! Since the night of Jesus' birth, I have known only joy. Everything is so much better now." Riel felt as if the little family were her own.

"We will never forget you, Riel, nor Kira or Josiah. You have made our stay in this stable bearable, and we owe you a great debt. Thank you for the swaddling cloth, Riel. I will always remember you when I place it around my baby."

"You will have to thank Broody; he is the one who contributed so much," Riel laughed as she gently rocked the baby Jesus in her arms. "Oh, Mary, I am the one indebted to you. To have witnessed things that prophets and kings longed for . . ." Riel's voice trailed off in wonder.

Joseph called from outside the stable, and in a few minutes the holy family was gone. Riel, Josiah, and Kira stood at the clearing and watched the humble travelers make their way down the inn's main path to the road.

The servants of the inn hated to see them go. All of them had witnessed incredible events that would stay with them forever. The birth of the child and all that had happened had changed the course of history for all those present on that night. The shepherds, the wise men, and the servants' lives had been eternally altered, and now they each must pursue the new course. Riel and Kira's own miracle remained in the making, and they needed to make preparations.

The huge barrel left by Saagi and her father had been pushed to the back of the storage area and covered with old rags. Kira and Riel didn't know what else to do. The knowledge of it being so close comforted Riel. It was a

The Swaddling Cloth

king's ransom, and neither Riel nor Kira knew what to do with it. In the night, before they fell asleep, they would often laugh and tease each other about what they would do, but the final serious decision would be left to Jude, they decided.

Riel remained in a state of disbelief that she would be the wife of Jude. She smiled every time she thought of the servant's description that night outside the stable, "You are the girl who loves the lambs." Her distinguishing attribute had been her love for the lamb, Broody. It was exciting yet terrifying to think that she would be the wife of the most talked-about young Jew in Bethlehem!

Alone on her long walks of carrying water each day, she would squeal with delight. The heavy vessels were no longer a burden; she felt no weight. For the first time since the death of her parents, she felt secure.

"Kira, when do you think he will come for me? What can I do to be ready?" she whispered late one night as Riel and the old cook sat by the fire, watching the embers die.

"I think the weaving you have done with the wool is a good start," Kira spoke, slowing as though her mind was somewhere else. "I never thought about it before now, but, Riel, you need a wedding garment."

"Where would I get that?" Riel spoke incredulously.

"The barrel!" whispered Kira with a newfound boldness. "Remember those fabrics? They were magnificent. Let's break the seal and look."

With slow and quiet motions, they delved into their treasures. By the light of the old oil lamp, Riel chose the cloth of her wedding garment. It was a soft blue fabric with spun gold woven throughout.

"Oh, Kira, it is fit for a queen!" she spoke reverently.

Then they looked at each and laughed until they cried.

"I will sew into the fabric the name of your father's tribe, Judah," declared Kira.

"Do you think we should? Is it right, with the circumstance of my birth?" Riel asked.

"Your father-in-law has declared you redeemed, Riel. Don't ever look back." Kira considered the subject of the past closed.

For weeks, the oil lamp could be seen burning in the inn late into the night, as an old mother of Israel prepared the garment for the bride.

Occasionally Riel would start to worry. "Did I dream it all? Was Ben-Jared overwhelmed by the birth of the holy child and spoke out of his head?"

Kira would look into the young woman's eyes with a calm assurance, and Riel would again be at peace. Fears could not stay where faith bloomed.

Crowds continued in the inn, and she worked as hard as ever, but Riel often made her way back to the stable, to the kind animals, and to the place where the precious baby had lain. As thrilled as she was at the thought of her marriage to Jude, it did not take away from what had happened in her heart the night she knelt before the new King. Her mind would return to that night of all nights, and she often found her thoughts turning to prayer.

"Jehovah, You were in this place! I saw You when I looked into Jesus' face. It was always hard to understand the prophet Isaiah when he said the Son would be 'The mighty God, The everlasting Father,' but I understand it! Lord God Jehovah! You became the Son, the Messiah! That you allowed me, a servant, a Samaritan, to witness the birth of the Messiah and all the miracles of that night,

The Swaddling Cloth

I cannot understand, but I am so happy You did.

"Right in the middle of Your great plans for the Christ child's birth, You did not fail to meet the needs of little Saagi. That was so gracious of You, Lord. You never forget the forgotten.

"And what You have done for me. . . ! Faith in Your mercy will never leave me. I am absolutely sure of one thing, You are directing the path of my life. You know that my heart is trembling concerning my shepherd, Jude, but I trust You to lead me. Help me not to be afraid. I know You will not forsake me and that I am never alone. Forgive me when I am afraid and my past grips me so tightly that I can't see Your plan. My hopes will forever be in you, Great Jehovah."

Riel's mind was being transformed. A blessed assurance was hers, not just from the anticipated future with Jude but from the peace that God had given her that night in the stable. The horrible uncertainty concerning her life faded each day. The fear of losing her place at the inn did not haunt her. Thinking about returning to the shepherd's life, living on the hills, and having a wonderful husband and family created an aura of joy that thrilled her.

Even Michal sensed the change in Riel. The fear in Riel that Michal had so often taken advantage of no longer existed. Michal was unsettled now. She avoided the servant girl who possessed such quiet confidence. Ben-Jared had spoken to Nathaniel about redeeming Riel, but the innkeeper had never mentioned the conversation to his daughter. It was too unbelievable. Nathaniel was taking Michal to Jerusalem and leaving the inn and everything associated with it. The future of the servants was of no concern to him. The innkeeper had quickly agreed to the sum Ben-Jared had offered. It was a ransom he could not refuse: one hundred sheep and one hundred shekels of silver. Nathaniel thought the chief shepherd had gone mad, but he intended to be gone before Ben-Jared could change his mind.

The low afternoon sun shone on a serene face as Riel lifted her water pot to make one more trip to the well of Bethlehem before sundown. Before her last walk each day, she would shyly and slowly make her way around to the front corner of the inn to look down the long, straight path to the main road at the entrance. When Jude came, it would most likely be at the end of the day. Kira had insisted they store oil for their lamps in case he called at night.

She could see a few travelers making their way to the inn. "I hope it is him. But if it is, I'm frightened to death," she laughed to herself but quickly saw the travelers were all strangers. She turned toward the back path to finish her day.

Bethlehem's well was alive with servants drawing water, and immediately Riel recognized the servants of Ben-Jared as they stood in the midst. Riel's secret completely changed her experiences at the well. The other servants still treated her with contempt, but the shield of a God who loved her and her future with Jude protected her from their unkindness. A Samaritan. They knew it and so did she, but now it didn't matter. God loved her, Kira and Josiah loved her, and a shepherd loved her.

The servants of Ben-Jared were just like the other servants, snubbing Riel when she approached the well. She kept her head down and got in the line to draw water. It still hurt to be ignored, but she knew something they didn't know. The feeling of belonging eased the pain. She

The Swaddling Cloth

was betrothed to their master, and that knowledge was a hedge.

Quietly, Riel stood remembering the innumerable times she had been in this very place alone and feeling so alone. She was alone today, but there was no sense of loneliness. She often thanked God for Kira and Josiah, knowing that they were a gift from God and had kept back the flood of sadness that threatened from time to time. But there was a different sort of feeling in her heart now that she had the love of Jude. It gave her amazing strength and joy that were impossible to describe. Her heart lifted to God a praise and a thanksgiving that all of heaven must have heard.

"Ben-Jared and Jude have been working night and day, preparing a place for the new couple, and it has just been completed. We are all leaving our tents and moving to new dwelling places," one young servant girl raised her voice as she spoke, capturing everyone's attention.

Riel placed both her hands over her heart and dropped her head. Such joy and happiness filled her that her whole body trembled. As quickly as she filled her clay pot, she headed back. Her steps had never been lighter, the glow of her countenance never brighter. "Working on a new place! Working on a new place! And it is finished!" The words of the servant echoed over and over in her mind.

She flung open the back door of the inn and announced to Kira, as laughter bubbled from her, "The waiting is over!"

Riel relayed the conversation she had overheard at the well, and Kira decided they would wait until they had served the evening meal to announce Riel's soon depar-

Riel and Jude

ture. The two servants threw themselves into the chore of serving the guests.

The earth was returning to its ancient hue of gray, but not before a magnificent sunset that served as a reminder to the world that the sun would be back tomorrow just as grand and glorious as ever. The silent hills once again looked on and made their quiet statement of everlasting strength.

Just as Riel and Kira finished placing the bowls on the main table, a shofar sounded outside the inn. The low, melancholy tone of the blowing of the ram's horn always carried significance.

Nathaniel threw open the door just as the cry went forth that all could hear, "The bridegroom is ready."

Ben-Jared and two elders of Bethlehem made their way into the inn. Everyone in the room seemed frozen in place. The travelers watched with interest, Nathaniel and Michal were shocked, and Kira and Riel were both terrified and thrilled.

"Ben-Jared! Welcome. We did not expect to see you. Ah, . . . ah. . . ." Nathaniel stammered, trying to think. "We are still . . . ah . . . still making preparations. Michal! Come!"

Ben-Jared stood in the doorway. The flicker of lamps burning in the night glowed behind him. His eyes scanned the room while he made his declaration. "Ten years ago, I cared more about the accumulation of wealth than about what was right. Your maidservant, Riel, is of my family. I am her kinsman redeemer, and I have come to buy her back. My son will take her as his bride," he spoke with a voice that would accept no compromise.

No one made a sound. The burning fire was the only thing in the room with courage to continue.

The Swaddling Cloth

Nathaniel, Michal, Josiah, and Kira turned to look at Riel. After a few seconds of glancing about the room, all eyes of the guests in the inn fastened on Riel. Michal's face was contorted with horror and contempt. She was afraid to speak, but anyone who knew Michal, knew she was raging.

"Nathaniel, I have given you one hundred of my finest sheep, one hundred shekels of silver, and I will double that amount if I may have the old woman, Kira," pronounced Ben-Jared.

Nathaniel's eyes widened with shock. Two hundred sheep and two hundred shekels of silver would make him a wealthy man. "Of course, anything for the house of Ben-Jared," he laughed loudly, rubbing his hands. "I'm not sure who will take care of the travelers if you take my two maidservants." The innkeeper was in a state of confusion, thinking of the silver and trying to converse at the same time.

"Will you accept my offer?" persisted Ben-Jared, who remained in the open doorway.

"Yes, yes, but now? Does the girl know of the marriage?" Nathaniel was unable to cover his disbelief.

Ben-Jared ignored Nathaniel and raised his gaze toward the food table, where Kira was standing. "My servants will carry your belongings to your new home," he addressed the old cook.

"Yes, my lord. We have only a simple barrel with our belongings," replied Kira, not raising her head.

Ben-Jared then looked to Riel but again addressed Nathaniel, "Also, my son has asked to buy one lamb of your flock." He paused. "The one of Riel's choosing."

Riel bowed low and marveled at the completeness of

Riel and Jude

her miracle, "Kind master, it would be the lamb, Broody." She glanced sideways at Josiah, whose eyes sparkled with tears.

"My lord," Josiah offered quickly, "I will fetch the lamb." He moved toward the back door.

Riel wanted to laugh, to dance, to sing! Everything her heart had ever desired now lay in her hand. She stood unsure of what to do, fearing to look at either Nathaniel or Michal. When Ben-Jared motioned for Riel to come, she moved swiftly toward him but suddenly stopped.

"My wedding garment. I must have it on before I see Jude. I will meet the wedding party on the main road."

Ben-Jared signaled his servant to place the silver on the table. As quickly as the three men appeared, they turned and were gone.

With that, Nathaniel turned to his guests and jovially declared, "The evening meal is ready. It may be awhile before we get another." He laughed nervously.

The guests, understanding little of what had transpired, made their way to the table.

"Kira, my heart is beating like a newborn child, and I can hardly breathe," Riel chattered in the food room as she hurriedly cleansed herself. Together they wrapped the wedding garment around the young bride.

"Our miracle continues, my little one."

A loud knock sounded at the back door. Kira and Riel looked at each other with immeasurable joy. Kira moved to answer it. There stood two young men dressed in white robes, newly sewn for the wedding celebration.

"We are servants of Jude, and we are here to carry your belongings," they spoke with their heads bowed, but there was a smile in their words.

The Swaddling Cloth

"Of course, come in. Come in. We were expecting you," Kira led them into the storage room where the barrel remained covered with rags. The seal was still intact because they had carefully cut it when they removed the cloth for the wedding garment. There was no question to whom the barrel belonged.

As the servants were leaving with the barrel tottering between them, Josiah arrived from the stable with Broody. He had attached a cord to the collar. Josiah paused, leaned on his staff, and watched the barrel move away, thanking God for His tender mercies. His mind went back to those early days when Riel had first come. With sorrow he had watched her go from a young shepherdess to a servant, and now with great happiness he was witnessing Riel's ascent from a servant to a woman of great standing. Who can predict what God will do?

"My little girl must feel like Queen Esther." His mind pondered the events of Saagi and the kings who had declared that they were of the lineage of Esther, the night of the Christ child's birth. "God moves in mysterious ways," he declared as he walked into the food room.

"Josiah, how I wish you could go with us. You have been so good and kind," spoke Riel gently as she embraced him.

"I know where the flocks of Jude and Ben-Jared roam. You will see much of this old shepherd," his eyes grew large with delight as he handed her the cord that held Broody. "You look like the queen of Israel," he laughed and cried as he held his precious girl tightly.

"Jehovah is so good to us, isn't He?" She spoke with great happiness as she straightened her garment and laughed, too. She breathed deeply and looked around the

Riel and Jude

food room for the last time. "Kira, I am ready."

Kira opened the curtain and glanced around the room where she had labored for so many years. She caught Nathaniel's eye and waved. He nodded his head but made no move to come to see them leave. It was just as well. There was nothing to say.

Michal sat by the fire, dreaming of her move to Jerusalem. The shock of Ben-Jared's announcement only made her more determined to leave Bethlehem as quickly as possible. Nothing ever happened in Bethlehem. She didn't need the house of Ben-Jared or its disgusting flocks.

Kira turned and followed Riel through the back door. The fire burned low and the mats were still leaning against the wall. She had no idea what would happen the next evening when there was no food prepared, but it wasn't her problem. They took nothing except the beaten old oil lamp that had lighted their darkness so many times.

As they came around the edge of the inn to the main entrance, they could see down the inn's path a group of people holding oil lamps. By now, Ben-Jared and the elders had joined the wedding party. The lamp that Kira held flickered a reply to their lights.

Riel went directly to Ben-Jared and bowed low to the earth, "Master, I . . ."

Ben-Jared interrupted her, "No longer call me Master, but Father."

Riel lifted her face and looked into the eyes of her kinsman redeemer. "Where is Jude?"

"He waits for you on a hill not far from here. He thought it best to meet you on the hills rather than at the inn," Ben-Jared said kindly. At that moment, Riel knew she once again had a father.

The Swaddling Cloth

The group began moving away with Ben-Jared leading. Riel and Kira followed. Joy and fear mingled in Riel's heart, and the only thing she knew to do was to cry out to God for help. Broody must have sensed her anxiousness, for he walked calmly beside her, not tugging at the cord.

When the wedding party turned onto the main road, the night was upon them and the stars sparkled in their grandeur. It seemed a thousand angels looked down upon them. The group had only walked a short distance when Ben-Jared turned to Riel and Kira and pointed to a hill just ahead.

"There is Jude."

A warm sense filled Riel's entire body as she looked up at the hills. There a small fire glowed in the night just a short distance from the road. Behind the dancing flames, stood a lone figure with a staff high above his head. The party halted, and Riel knew the time had come to meet her bridegroom.

She turned to embrace Kira.

"Let me take the lamb. He might wrinkle your garment," Kira spoke in a low yet excited voice.

"No," she shook her head and glanced again at the top of the hill, "I want Broody to go with me."

So amidst the beloved hills, the young bride walked to meet her bridegroom with one attendant, the lamb. Her eyes were shining, not only with the glow of the starlit heavens but also with the light of happiness that fills the eyes of those who love completely.

When Jude saw a single lamp leave the others and move toward him, he hastily covered his fire. With only his staff, he strode down the hillside with the grace that comes to a shepherd of those hills. When the shepherd's staff met the single flickering light at the midpoint of the hill, Riel bowed herself low, "My lord, I am Riel, the girl who loves the lambs."

He lifted her head with one hand and then took her hand, drawing her close to him. The fragrance of the wind, fire, and the hills met her as she came close to him. Jude looked straight into her eyes and did not alter his gaze as he spoke. "Riel, I have loved you since I first saw you months ago. My love grew each time I heard you laugh; each time your voice reached my ears. And then to think that together we would see the star and the holy child, Jesus! When I saw you that marvelous night, there in the stable, I knew I had found the one who had played and sang on the hillside all those months ago, the one I loved."

The bride's eyes stayed fixed on his in the pure delight of having the undivided attention of one she honored so greatly. "I never dreamed anyone listened," she broke from his eyes and looked at Broody standing quietly beside them.

Jude ran his hand over the soft head of the lamb; then he gently placed both his hands on Riel's shoulders and looked directly into her eyes. "You are exactly as I imagined when I first heard you that late evening. When I came to the inn to speak with Nathaniel, I should have known immediately."

The weight of his hands on her shoulders and the earnestness in his voice deeply affected her. She possessed the love of this wonderful man. She knew at that moment she would love this shepherd until she took her last breath.

Riel interrupted. "It does not matter now. God has directed our steps."

The Swaddling Cloth

Jude glanced at the wedding party that waited for them at the road. "Yes, I know that God has been with us, and the misunderstanding about Michal is not important. And that you were made a servant for that brutish man, Nathaniel, my father will try to make up for, as long as he lives."

Jude shook his head as though to clear his mind. "But I want to say something, and then it will never be mentioned again."

He continued with that undivided attention that made Riel's heart leap with delight. "My father explained to me the circumstances of your birth. It doesn't make any difference to me, and it never will. It will never be spoken of again in the house of Ben-Jared or in the house of Jude. Those who gathered at the manger that night are the favored of the earth."

Riel's voice shook with emotion, and tears ran down her face. "God has brought us together. How can I ever repay Him for what He has brought to my life? Jude, you are my gift from God, and I will never stop loving you."

Jude took Broody's cord in one hand and Riel's hand in his other. The three walked down the hill and joined the others.

The bridegroom laughed when he saw the large barrel being lifted again as they started out. Three servants were trying to carry the bulky load.

"You're not trying to take all of Nathaniel's paying customers away in that barrel, are you?" he teased his bride.

"No," replied Kira with a twinkle in her eye and a glance toward the embarrassed Riel. "That is a wedding gift from a king."

"Oh, yes, of course," Jude exclaimed in jest, thinking the old servant was teasing back with him. "Everyone knows this is the most important wedding in Bethlehem!" he spoke playfully. "Some of the shepherds told that there were some kings who came through around here." Jude placed his arm around Kira and patted her shoulder while he held onto Riel's hand, with Broody dancing between them.

Happy and joyful remarks were made as they made their way to the camp of Ben-Jared. After a short distance, the young couple with their lamb had dropped back a little distance from the others. Jude wanted to tell her of their newly finished home, the first one for the tent-dwelling shepherds. But he promised her that they would always keep a tent to take out on the hills, and Riel was overcome with pleasure.

The wedding party stopped at the crest of a hill and looked down at the place where the house of Ben-Jared camped. The wedding feast awaited them, with torches aflame and glowing in the night. As Jude and Riel walked up to the rest of the group, they all paused and looked down at the beautiful sight.

Ben-Jared spoke as he placed his arm around his son, "Riel, welcome to the house of Ben-Jared, shepherds of Israel, shepherds to the Messiah."

He raised his arm toward the camp and the sea of flocks that surrounded it. All the shepherds had returned for this time of celebration. "This now belongs to you and Jude. First the wedding, and then the feast. My wife awaits us."

Riel looked down at the firelit valley, and then her eyes glanced back toward the direction they had come. There were her beloved hills, resting quietly, waiting for the sun to shine again. She could still make out their

The Swaddling Cloth

blackened silhouettes though it was growing late. Their loveliness was not just in their peaks but also in their valleys. The memory of her own valleys would always be tucked away in the recesses of her mind. Those low places had molded her character.

As her mind went back to the difficult times, she suddenly lifted her gaze. There, reigning in the darkness of the night and making the hills seem so small, were the eternal stars, endless in number. No matter how many valleys there had been, reigning above them all were the tiny lamps of God, beaming out hope in a blackened sea. The light of God had never gone out.

Jude gently put his arm around Riel and looked deeply into her eyes. "There will never be a day when you are not loved and cherished. God has given me the wife for whom I have longed. He has placed you in my care, and I swear before God this night that I will honor, protect, and love you as long as I live."

Riel could not find words to speak, but her eyes told him of her deep and abiding love. Jude took her hand and led her to their marriage feast to celebrate their love, their marriage, and to give glory to the only wise God who had worked out the divine plan for their lives. In the midst of the greatest event in human history, God was at work in the life of a young woman who thought she was insignificant.

Afterword

A fascinating event, concerning Jesus Christ, is recorded in the Gospel of John:

John 4:4 *And he must needs go through Samaria.*

Jesus *had* to go through Samaria! There was something about Samaria that drew the Savior. Most Jews would never have considered walking through that area because there were deep-seated prejudices against the Samaritan people by the Jews. But Jesus seemed to be compelled to go there. He met a woman and gave her the gospel message, changing forever her life and the city she lived in. (See John 4.)

I suddenly realized that besides reaching out to this woman, at other times Jesus reached out to this sect of people during His ministry and later during the times of the apostles:

- He healed lepers who were Samaritans (Luke 17).
- He used a Samaritan as the exemplar when he told the parable about reaching out to the hurting (Luke 10). In fact, today we know it as the parable of the Good Samartian.
- When Jesus told His disciples to take the gospel to the world, Samaria was specifically included (Acts 1:8).
- Acts 8 records the events that took place when the gospel was preached in Samaria. The Holy Ghost was given to the Samaritans when Peter and John laid hands on them. Also, there are two

other references in Acts to the gospel being preached in Samaria (Acts 9 and Acts 15).

So it is not without foundation that we can conclude Jesus had a special place in His heart for this group of people. Maybe, just maybe, there was a Samaritan who moved the heart of God and caused special consideration to be given to this outcast group of people. Maybe there really was a Riel.